JEDI APPRENTICE

The Day of Reckoning

Jude Watson

D1023180

LUCAS BOOKS

SCHOLASTIC INC.

New York Toronto London Auckland Sydney
Mexico City New Delhi Hong Kong

ISBN 0-590-52079-2

12 11 10 9 8 7 6 5 4 3 2 1   0 1 2 3 4 5 6/0

Printed in the U.S.A.
First Scholastic printing, June 2000

CHAPTER 1

The sleek spaceliner *Leviathan* was jammed with passengers. Every stateroom was full. The lounges and seating areas swirled with color and noise as people from many worlds conversed, ate, argued, laughed, and played games of chance to pass the time.

Obi-Wan Kenobi sat and observed it all. As a Jedi on missions to other worlds, he sometimes got a glimpse of lavish surroundings, but this was his first trip on a luxury spaceliner. He longed to explore the many amusements on board — the game room, the interactive hologram suite, the eating areas with their array of foods and sweets. There was no reason he could not. His companion and former Jedi Master, Qui-Gon Jinn, had told him to feel free to explore. But Obi-Wan did not want to leave his side.

Next to him, Qui-Gon seemed not to notice

his surroundings. The Jedi Knight had picked a corner seat in the spacious lounge. His chair faced outward toward the throng. It was a position the Jedi often chose, for it allowed observation without interaction. But Qui-Gon Jinn only made obligatory sweeps of the crowd in order to ascertain potential danger or disturbance before returning his attention to the datapad in his lap. He spent his time studying the information about the mission ahead that Jedi Knight Tahl had managed to gather back at the Temple on Coruscant.

Their mission was unofficial. Against the wishes of the Jedi Council, they were heading to the home planet of Xanatos, the enemy who had tried to destroy the Jedi Temple.

Qui-Gon was still brooding about the escape of Xanatos, Obi-Wan knew. Anger was not an appropriate emotion for a Jedi, but Obi-Wan sensed Qui-Gon's taut frustration. He had faced Xanatos in battle, and had been forced to let his opponent escape in order to save the Temple.

Obi-Wan knew that moment still haunted Qui-Gon. He had come close to stopping Xanatos. It made him even more determined to bring him to justice now. Qui-Gon felt strongly that Xanatos was a grave threat to the galaxy while on the loose.

Obi-Wan knew that Qui-Gon took this mission

personally. Xanatos had once been Qui-Gon's Jedi apprentice, just as Obi-Wan had.

And we both betrayed him, Obi-Wan thought.

His offense, he knew, was not even close to what Xanatos had done. The dark side preyed on Xanatos. He lusted after power and wealth. His every decision moved him closer to the heart of evil.

Obi-Wan had betrayed Qui-Gon by abandoning him. He had decided to leave the Jedi order to stay to help a planet regain peace. He had come to regret the decision. The Council had agreed that he could rejoin the Jedi, but he was now on probation. Obi-Wan could regain what he had, but he could not seem to regain Qui-Gon's trust. Something essential between them had been violated. Now they were just feeling their way along. On this mission, Obi-Wan hoped to show Qui-Gon that they could restore the bond they had started to form.

The Council had not forbidden him to accompany Qui-Gon — they allowed him to go. Still, his decision had not pleased them. They already had a problem with what they saw as his impulsive decision to leave the Jedi. This latest decision hadn't changed their opinion.

Obi-Wan had to admit that he was relieved to be temporarily out from under the Council's scrutiny as well as the Temple itself. In the final battle, a Jedi student had fallen to his death in front of him. Obi-Wan had not been responsible. Why did the death continue to haunt him? When he had taken off from the Temple grounds, a heaviness had seemed to lift from his heart.

Qui-Gon had considered many ways to enter the planet without detection, but finally decided the simplest way was best. They would arrive among a throng, as tourists.

Telos was a rich planet with many natural beauties. It had a thriving tourist trade and business interests with other planets in the galaxy. Transports were always crowded.

The many travelers made it easy for the Jedi to disappear. They wore nondescript brown cloaks over their tunics and kept their lightsabers hidden. Although Qui-Gon was a powerfully built man with noble features, he was also capable of dimming his presence and folding into a crowd. Obi-Wan followed his example. They were not recognizable as Jedi, and no one paid the slightest attention to them. Obi-Wan settled back into the plush upholstery and watched as a group of Duros walked by, all speaking in Basic.

"This is my third trip," one of them said. "You're going to love Katharsis."

"They won't let outsiders into the final

round," the other said. "That's where you can really score."

Obi-Wan wondered what Katharsis was. Some kind of game? He missed the other's reply, for Qui-Gon had looked up from his datapad at last.

"I think the weak link is UniFy," he said. "We'll start there."

Obi-Wan nodded. UniFy was a Telosian company that the Jedi Master Tahl suspected was a front for Offworld, the huge mining corporation that spanned the galaxy. Xanatos headed the company. No one knew where the headquarters were.

Qui-Gon's brows came together in a frown as he gazed at Obi-Wan. Obi-Wan had no idea what he was thinking. Was he worrying about the mission ahead, or was he regretting Obi-Wan's presence?

They had lost the connection they had once had. There had been fitful starts and shaky periods in their Master–Padawan relationship from the beginning. Still, there had been many times when Obi-Wan knew what Qui-Gon would ask before he asked it. And Qui-Gon often knew exactly what Obi-Wan was feeling without his having to say a word.

Now Obi-Wan felt a void.

He would be able to feel connected to Qui-

Gon again, he told himself. It would just take time. Back at the Temple, the last expression of good-bye from his friend Bant had been one simple word: *patience.*

Obi-Wan and Qui-Gon hadn't had time to resolve anything. They hadn't had time to argue, or replay their decisions. The flurry of departure had consumed them. There had been information to gather, supplies to pack, and good-byes to be said.

The spaceliner drew closer to the towers of Thani, the capital city of Telos. It flew into a landing bay and docked with the gentlest of bumps. The public-address system announced that arrival procedures were now underway.

They stood and gathered their packs, then joined the stream of passengers heading for the exit.

Qui-Gon leaned in to speak to Obi-Wan softly. "No doubt he will be hard to find," he said. "He knows that I will pursue him. We will have to flush him out."

The announcement system informed them in a pleasant tone that there would be a slight delay in disembarking. Identification would be checked by security police on Telos. Everyone would have to be cleared before leaving the ship.

Passengers began to grumble. Why were security procedures suddenly so stringent? This would take time. They were anxious to reach their destinations.

"I hear they're checking for some escaped criminals," someone said near Obi-Wan's elbow. "Bad luck for all of us."

Through the crowd, Obi-Wan glimpsed the security police herding the passengers into orderly lines. Qui-Gon frowned.

"I wanted to slip in unobserved," he said. "If they discover we are Jedi, it could tip off Xanatos. Tahl said he has bribed many officials here."

With a slight movement of his head, Qui-Gon signaled to Obi-Wan. It was time for them to find their own exit.

CHAPTER 2

"Where are we going?" Obi-Wan asked as they moved fluidly through the pressing throng.

"When a big spaceliner docks, the kitchens have to receive new shipments of food," Qui-Gon remarked. "When you want to leave someplace unobserved, pick the busiest spot."

Obi-Wan followed Qui-Gon down several levels to the service area. Qui-Gon always explored any large transport soon after boarding. He knew where the tech and service levels were as well as all exits from the spaceliner. "Remember, Obi-Wan," he had said, "if you are heading to a dangerous mission, the danger can begin before you are ready for it. Be prepared."

The scent of roasting meat and baking bread filled Obi-Wan's nostrils as they passed the kitchens. His stomach rumbled. Why was it that even during a hasty escape, he could still feel hungry? He was glad when the smells dissipated as they slipped into the storage areas.

Qui-Gon hurried past shelves and bins full of food until he came to the door that led to the loading bay. He glanced through the window to make sure there were no security personnel before accessing the door. It hissed open, and they stepped out onto the loading bay.

Workers were busily unloading supplies onto small gravsleds. A large hauler stood outside the ship, its port bay door yawning open.

"Grab a container," Qui-Gon instructed as he bent down to hoist a box marked DRIED FRUIT.

Obi-Wan picked up a bin at his feet marked SOLI GRAINS. He let out an *oof* as he hoisted it to his shoulder. Why couldn't he have picked something light, as Qui-Gon had?

Quickly Qui-Gon strode toward the hauler. No one seemed to notice that they were carrying items out of the ship, not in. One of Qui-Gon's many lessons to Obi-Wan had been that if you looked busy in an unfamiliar environment, you were often ignored.

They made it to the hauler without anyone giving them a glance. Obi-Wan put down his heavy bin with relief near the stacks of cartons and boxes. From here they could see the busy port station. Passengers who had been cleared were milling around, bargaining for local transportation. Qui-Gon and Obi-Wan strolled toward them.

"You there! Stop!" The harsh command came from behind them.

"Don't turn," Qui-Gon told Obi-Wan in a soft voice. "Act as though you don't know who they're talking to."

"Stop!" The sound of running feet came from behind them.

Obi-Wan saw a split second of indecision on Qui-Gon's part. They had done nothing wrong. There was no reason to run. Yet they would have to give explanations Qui-Gon was not willing to give.

Qui-Gon made the decision in his usual swift fashion. "Run," he said crisply.

Obi-Wan had been expecting the command. He shot forward with Qui-Gon. The two Jedi moved as lightly as a breeze, slipping in and out of the crowd without jostling an elbow or bumping a shoulder. Only a whisper of air might disturb a cloak or a tendril of hair as they shot by.

They reached the entrance to the terminal and joined the stream of strollers on the city streets. Immediately Qui-Gon slowed his pace in order to melt into the crowd. Obi-Wan followed suit, carefully controlling his breathing.

He admired Qui-Gon's ability to switch from a full-tilt run to a casual pace without missing a beat. To any observer, Qui-Gon appeared to be a casual walker on the city streets.

The streets were even more crowded than the terminal. "No doubt they'll give up," Qui-Gon said to Obi-Wan, nodding and smiling as though he were remarking on the weather. "It's a tedious job tracking a couple of stray travelers through the city streets."

With his heartbeat and nerves returning to normal, Obi-Wan was now able to observe his surroundings. The city of Thani was bustling. Landspeeders clogged the wide boulevard. Buildings hundreds of meters high rose on either side. Their different façades flashed silver and bronze in the bright sunlight. Crowded between the tall, impressive buildings were smaller structures. Blinking readout signs advertised loans at low rates, or credits advanced against goods. Disorderly lines snaked out from these buildings, the people jostling to get inside. Obi-Wan passed a large billboard that read: WEALTH BEYOND IMAGINING IS JUST ONE BET AWAY: KATHARSIS

"Katharsis," he repeated. "I heard that name on the spaceliner."

"I've never heard of it. Thani has changed since I was here last," Qui-Gon mused. "Of course it was almost ten years ago. It seems bigger, noisier. And something else is different about it now. . . ."

Obi-Wan suddenly caught a flicker of movement behind him. He glanced at the shiny façade of the next building. Two navy-suited security police officers were swiftly making their way forward, attracting little attention on the busy street. There was no doubt in Obi-Wan's mind that they were heading for them.

"Qui-Gon —" he started, but Qui-Gon had already seen them.

"They are more determined than I thought," he said, picking up his pace. "Go left."

Obi-Wan wheeled to his left down a narrow alley. They moved quickly now, running down the alley, using the Force to leap over a pile of abandoned crates, and turning sharply right into another alley.

Blaster fire pinged behind them. They heard the sound of exploding crates peppering the wall.

"They mean business," Qui-Gon said. "We'd better go up."

The security police were still out of sight, but they'd round the corner in a few seconds. Qui-Gon reached for the liquid-cable launcher on his belt. He activated the device, and the dual-strand cord shot upward and hooked around the lip of a rooftop overhead. Obi-Wan activated his own liquid-cable. They held on and let the device carry them up to the rooftop, leaping up and landing on their feet. Quickly, they retracted the cords.

Qui-Gon watched as the security police ran down the alley. They ran past the rooftop, turned a corner, and disappeared.

"That's a relief," Obi-Wan said.

But Qui-Gon did not move. A few seconds later, the security police returned. One of them took out a pair of electrobinoculars and began sweeping the rooftops.

"They're not giving up, I'm afraid," Qui-Gon remarked mildly.

The two Jedi moved backward quickly on their hands and knees until they were out of range. Then they jumped from the opposite side of the roof down to the pavement. They ran down a short stretch of the alley and spilled out into the crowded street again.

"We'll never lose them this way," Qui-Gon said.

Obi-Wan craned his neck and looked over the heads of the surging crowd. "Everyone is heading toward that dome," he said to Qui-Gon. "Maybe we can lose them inside."

They joined the crowd, weaving through it in order to make it to the entrance quickly. A giant sign flashed in letters a hundred meters high: K A T H A R S I S.

"I guess we're about to find out what it is," Obi-Wan said curiously.

There were several entrances, and Qui-Gon joined the line at the most crowded. The stream of people pushed through an opening that was big enough to fly a starfighter through.

NEED CREDITS? STOP HERE! The signs flashed around a row of booths near the entrance. Farther on Obi-Wan saw food stalls. Tempting aromas floated toward them. His stomach rumbled again. He almost groaned. With Qui-Gon, he never knew when his next meal would come. His former Jedi Master seemed to exist on a diet of fresh air and determination.

"This must be some sort of gambling event," Qui-Gon said. "Curious."

"And popular," Obi-Wan added, jostled by the surging crowd.

As they entered the interior of the dome, they found themselves high above the central area, which was one giant ring with a smaller concentric ring inside. Large screens were hung at various heights and distances around the dome so that they were visible throughout the giant space. Scenes of natural beauty flashed across them while booming music played out of hidden speakers.

Floating boxes surrounded the central wings. Stationary seating ringed the area, the topmost rows lost in the vastness of the dome.

They climbed up, searching for two empty seats near exits. Qui-Gon's keen gaze swept the crowd below them, looking for the security police who had been following them.

At last he found places a few seats in from the end. They sat, and Obi-Wan turned his attention to the giant screens, which began to flash a stream of names and numbers he could not decipher. There was also a screen with a keypad built into his armrest.

While Qui-Gon kept his eyes on the crowd, Obi-Wan leaned over to a tall Telosian seated next to him.

"This is my first time here," he said. "Can you explain what's going on?"

"The screens are flashing the current odds for the games," his seatmate replied, pointing. "You can bet at your seat on each event. There are twenty contestants competing in a variety of contests."

"Last week Rolo was maimed," his companion said dolefully. "I bet twenty thousand credits on him."

The Telosian's clothes were threadbare. He hardly looked like a rich citizen. Obi-Wan was shocked. How could he afford to bet so much?

"Today my money is on Tamor," the second Telosian continued.

"You can place larger bets as the day goes on," the first Telosian explained. "Then for the last contest we all drop out and the lottery bettors get to play."

"The lottery bettors?" Obi-Wan asked.

He nodded. "Every citizen is entered in a lottery each week. Three are chosen. They're the only ones who can bet on the last contest. The pot is enormous."

"You're set for life if you win," his companion said, his eyes glowing. "Last week no one won, so it's bigger than ever."

"The lottery is free," the first Telosian explained. "Every native Telosian is entered automatically by the government. It's a great thing for Telos."

Really? Obi-Wan wondered, looking around at the crowd. Now he understood the ferocious energy he felt pulsing through the crowd, uniting it. It was greed.

"It seems as though the entire city is here," Obi-Wan remarked.

The two Telosians nodded. "The city empties into the dome on Katharsis Day. And others come from all over the planet."

"There are Katharsis domes in other parts of

Telos, of course," the second Telosian said. "But this is the biggest," he added proudly.

"It's beginning! I have to place my bet." The first Telosian swiveled to face the center of the dome. His avid eyes searched the contestants.

The crowd began to roar as the competitors took their places in the ring below. They lined up and bowed to the crowd.

Obi-Wan felt Qui-Gon stiffen slightly. The Jedi Knight's eyes were directed several levels down. Obi-Wan followed his gaze. The same security officers were walking up and down the rows, their eyes constantly moving.

"Telosian security must be commended," Qui-Gon remarked as he stood. "They certainly are thorough."

Obi-Wan followed Qui-Gon as they eased their way past the bettors in the row. When they reached the aisle they picked up their pace, climbing steadily past the next section, and the next. Behind them, the security officers continued to climb, their eyes sweeping the crowd.

"We'll have to circle around down to an exit level," Qui-Gon told Obi-Wan over the roar of applause.

Obi-Wan scanned the area ahead for the blue-lighted exit signs. He saw one ahead and pointed it out to Qui-Gon. But when they reached it, they saw that it had been blocked off. If the door opened, an alarm would sound.

Qui-Gon turned back the way they had come, but the security police were now cruising the rows next to them. Any moment they would spot the Jedi.

"I don't know if they're pursuing us, or looking for those escaped criminals," Qui-Gon said, frowning. "I guess we're going to have to find out. I'll use the Force to bluff our way through."

At that moment, one of the security officers looked over the heads of the crowd and spotted them. He nudged his companion and they started toward the Jedi, moving swiftly and quietly so as not to attract attention.

Suddenly, a friendly voice came from behind them. "You two need some seats? I've got plenty of room in my box."

They looked over. A young man sat in one of the luxury floating boxes. It was still anchored to the side. His dark eyes beamed at them in a friendly way and his sandy hair was rumpled as though he passed his hands through it frequently.

"Care to join me?" he asked.

"Thank you. We'd be honored to accept," Qui-Gon responded, stepping into the box. Without seeming to hurry, he motioned for Obi-Wan to do the same.

Obi-Wan eased into the box with the same swiftness. Their new companion pressed a lever, and the box suddenly detached from the floor and zoomed out into the center of the dome.

"Thank you *again*," Qui-Gon said politely. "It was hard for us to find a place to sit."

"Sure." Their rescuer gave them a shrewd look. "Especially when you're being chased by security police. If you think you're safe with me, you're crazy."

CHAPTER 3

The young man burst out laughing before they could respond. "Joke!" he cried. "If you ask me, the security police don't have enough to do. We don't have much of a crime problem here on Telos, so they run after you if you toss away a muja pit. Even innocent folks like me get stopped all the time. I ask you, do I look like a bad guy?" He shrugged and pointed to his chest, smiling.

"No," Obi-Wan said politely, even though he had learned in his limited experience that evil came in many forms.

Their companion laughed again and turned to Qui-Gon. "Your companion lies well. That's a good skill."

"He did not lie," Qui-Gon answered. "You don't appear to be bad, it's true. But neither do you appear to be good. Our acquaintance is too short to make such a judgment."

Their rescuer looked from Qui-Gon to Obi-Wan, a delighted grin on his face. "Whoa, did I hit the jackpot. What a couple of smart guys. Do you know how to bet against the odds?"

"No," Qui-Gon said with a smile. "We're too smart for that."

This time, their rescuer roared with laughter. "Joke! Do I know how to pick friends, I ask you? By the way, my name is Denetrus. You can call me Den."

"Pleased to meet you," Qui-Gon responded. "I am Qui-Gon Jinn and this is Obi-Wan Kenobi."

"Tourists?"

"We're here on business," Qui-Gon answered.

"Lots of business here on Telos," Den said. "I'm a tech worker, so I've been fired from the best of them." He flashed them a cheerful grin.

"Have you ever worked for UniFy?" Qui-Gon asked.

"Sure, who hasn't? They're the biggest employer on Telos. They hire contract workers all the time. Is that why you're here?"

"No," Qui-Gon said carefully. "We just have a meeting there."

Den nodded. "They're a powerful company." He waved his arm to indicate the giant screens around them that flashed images of the global parks and natural beauties of Telos. "UniFy is restoring our natural parks. Most of the proceeds from Katharsis are used for maintaining and preserving the land. The government set it up when the people protested our high taxes. Now we pay hardly any taxes at all. Katharsis saved us from that. Not to mention that it makes us all rich beyond our dreams."

"But only if you win," Qui-Gon pointed out.

"Oh, but all of us here plan to win," Den said, lifting an ironic eyebrow. "Take me. I'm sure this is my lucky day."

They turned toward the smaller center ring of the dome, where a platform was rising up through the floor into the air, creating a dais. A tall white-haired man stood on it, raising his arms to the crowd.

"That's the treasurer of Telos, Vox Chun," Den told them over the roar of the crowd.

A chill passed through Obi-Wan, and he exchanged a quick glance with Qui-Gon. Vox Chun was the father of the student who had fought with Obi-Wan and plunged to his death. Bruck Chun had been a Jedi student who had fallen under the influence of Xanatos. Obi-Wan had battled him, trying to save his friend Bant. Bruck had lost his balance and fallen. Obi-Wan had reached for him and grabbed empty air. The fall had broken Bruck's neck. Obi-Wan closed his eyes, remembering the shock of that moment. When he opened them, Qui-Gon was looking at him with compassion.

"The games can't begin without some big-head getting up and droning on about his own accomplishments," Den continued. "It's a good time to take a nap."

Quickly, Obi-Wan returned his attention to the present. He did not mean to forget the past, but he could not let it distract him. "Welcome, Telosians and friends from the galaxy!" Vox Chun shouted. A roar answered him. He waited it out, smiling, then held up a hand. "Thanks to each one of you, the natural beauties of our beloved Telos are being preserved!"

Another roar erupted, this one more deafening than the last. Music swelled from the speakers, and a message flashed against a stunning picture of steam eruptions along a glittering blue shore: KATHARSIS PROTECTS OUR SACRED SPACES.

"If there is no winner today, at the next Katharsis the grand lottery prize will be the largest ever awarded on Telos!" Chun continued. He waited out the cheers and held up a hand. "In honor of this event, the first citizen of Telos will present the prize. Our great good friend, our most beloved benefactor, the most trusted man on Telos — Xanatos!"

Qui-Gon gave a start as the dome erupted in

loud cheers. Den watched it all, his lips curving in the ironic smile he seemed to wear at all times. Spotlights played over the dome and then centered on a front floating box. A tall man stood and waved.

It was Xanatos.

Qui-Gon watched in disbelief as the crowd stamped its feet and thundered, "XANATOS, XANATOS!" over and over.

Qui-Gon had thought he'd prepared for any twist, any sudden reversal. He had not prepared for this. Xanatos was not in hiding. He didn't need to be. It was obvious that he was loved by the people of Telos.

But why? Qui-Gon wondered. Xanatos had been a traitor. Less than ten years before, he had conspired with his father to drain the planet's treasury. He had schemed to involve Telos in a needless, destructive war with a neighboring planet. The people must have been manipulated or lied to, for how could they ignore how he had schemed to plunge them into war?

He felt Obi-Wan stir by his side. The boy was just as shocked as he was. He admired how Obi-Wan kept his voice steady and his expression only mildly curious as he turned to Den.

"Who is this Xanatos?" he asked.

"Our most beloved benefactor," Den mimicked, then shrugged. "He's done a lot for Telos."

"I think I've heard of his father, Crion," Qui-Gon remarked casually. "Wasn't he governor of Telos once?"

Den nodded. "He was involved in a scandal. His enemies claimed he was trying to start a war with a neighboring planet in order to enrich himself. But Xanatos investigated and proved it wasn't true. Most Telosians consider both of them heroes."

Den turned back to the central ring as Vox Chun entered a floating box and the first contest began. The contestants ringed the interior space of the dome. All of them rode swoops.

"The first game is called Obstacle," Den explained. "Holograms of obstacles are hurtled at the swoops in an escalating pattern. The object is to avoid them — and the other contestants. It takes superior flying skills. Do you want to place a bet?"

Qui-Gon shook his head. "I think we'll just watch for today, Den."

"Just like I said before," Den muttered, already placing his bet. "You guys are smart."

Qui-Gon was startled at the ferocity of the contests. The crowd seemed happiest when the contestants were in great danger. When two swoops collided, a dark energy swirled inside the giant dome. When one contestant was carried out on a stretcher, the crowd screamed in delight. It was a disturbing event.

Telos had been a peaceful planet, renowned for its innovative tech industry and its interest in culture and the arts. Qui-Gon wondered what had happened. Had Katharsis changed them, or had their years of prosperity dulled their senses and made them long for more bloodthirsty, pulse-pounding pleasures?

Den seemed unmoved by the commotion around him. He carried a small datapad and entered numbers, constantly watching the odds. Qui-Gon could see he was a serious gambler, yet he placed very small bets.

At last a break was called. The third round of the contest consisted of a vibroblade duel as the contestants were strung from tension cords. The vibroblades did not cut but carried a small electrical charge. The duel had been a free-for-all. Three more contestants had dropped out. One had been seriously injured. The remaining group looked exhausted and drained. Yet after the break they would have to undergo another grueling set of contests.

"Hungry? We can head to the food stalls,"

Den said, activating the floating box to return to the stadium platform.

"Thank you, but I think we'll move on," Qui-Gon said politely. "We must tend to our business. Can you direct us to UniFy?"

"You can't miss it — just keep heading down the main boulevard. It's on your left. Good luck," Den told them.

They bowed and joined the sea of beings heading for the food stalls in the middle tier of the dome. The security police were nowhere in sight. Qui-Gon hoped they'd given up at last. As the crowd surged toward the tempting food, Qui-Gon and Obi-Wan headed toward the blue-lighted exit.

As they passed by the vast arching struts that held up the dome, Qui-Gon felt a sudden surge in the dark side of the Force. Alarmed, he stopped and faded back into the shadow of a thick durasteel strut. Obi-Wan had felt the surge as well and moved with him.

Qui-Gon gave his surroundings a sweeping glance. He knew what he was looking for.

A black shape detached from a shadowy passageway entrance. Xanatos strode across the empty space, the deep blue lining of his dark cape swirling around him, his black hair flowing to his shoulders. Suddenly, he stopped.

As a former Jedi, Xanatos was also Force-sensitive. He had stopped so abruptly that Qui-Gon had no doubt that he had felt the presence of the two Jedi. But would he interpret what he felt to mean that Qui-Gon was near?

Xanatos stood in the harsh overhead light. The scar that formed a half-circle on his cheek stood out, whiter than his pale, translucent skin. He surveyed the crowd a few meters away as they surged toward the food stalls. His gaze moved slowly over each form. Then he stopped and turned. His eyes swept the empty space, the arching struts, the corridors leading out in all directions.

Qui-Gon did not move. He did not even breathe. Obi-Wan was trying to be just as still beside him. Not with the flicker of an eyelash would they disturb the deep shadows.

Xanatos did not see them. But a slow smile spread over his face.

Qui-Gon knew what the smile meant. Xanatos knew they were here.

The battle had begun.

CHAPTER 4

Chuckling, Xanatos swiveled and strode back into the central dome.

"He knows we're here," Obi-Wan said quietly.

"Yes," Qui-Gon agreed. "Let's find UniFy. We must move as quickly as we can."

They left the dome and started down the main boulevard. The streets were strangely deserted. Qui-Gon imagined that most of the population was in the Katharsis Dome. Did they suspend work during Katharsis days?

He and Obi-Won passed a large, impressive building with blue-veined stone columns in front. A silver plaque read THE XANATOS INSTITUTE FOR HEALING.

"He has certainly made his mark," Qui-Gon murmured.

"Look at the library across the street," Obi-Wan said, pointing. "He funded that, too."

"The problem will not be finding him, obviously," Qui-Gon said. "The challenge will be to expose him for what he really is. The people love him. He has made sure of that. He has protected himself better by staying in the open than by hiding."

Obi-Wan scanned a sign that announced that Xanatos was providing the funds to restore a large city park. "He must have a reason behind all this," he observed.

"He always has a reason," Qui-Gon agreed. "Naturally he wants to exert influence on Telos. But that is too broad a goal for him. We shall have to discover exactly what he intends."

"Hey, genius guys!"

They turned to see Den heading for them. "I thought you might need help finding UniFy," he said. "I realized that there's no sign on the building."

"What about the lottery?" Obi-Wan asked. "Isn't today your lucky day?"

"All my days are lucky, kid," Den said, falling into step next to them. "But I don't get a chance to do a good deed often enough."

"We were just noticing all the buildings Xanatos has built in Thani," Qui-Gon remarked. "He has been a true benefactor."

Den waved an arm. "In the past few years he's supported parks, libraries, med centers, the big healing institute — he's made a fortune in mining throughout the galaxy, but he doesn't hoard it. He spreads it around. That's more than any of those lottery winners will do, let me tell you."

They passed one of the pale blue information kiosks. Qui-Gon glanced at the information board on the front. To his shock, he saw his own face.

"Is this the main park in Thani?" he asked Den, sweeping an arm to the opposite side of the street, where a path beckoned beneath spreading trees.

Den turned away, as Qui-Gon had hoped he would. "No, it's one of the smaller ones. The largest is on the east side of the city."

The diversion gave Qui-Gon enough time to study the notice on the wall. After his picture faded on the screen, Obi-Wan's appeared. WANTED. GALACTIC CRIMINALS. REWARD. He read the words in a flash.

So that was why the security police hadn't given up!

There could be only one explanation: Xanatos. He had arranged this. Now Qui-Gon understood his smile. He knew that it was only a matter of time before Qui-Gon and Obi-Wan were captured.

Even as he walked and exchanged conversation with Den, Qui-Gon's mind sifted through his options. Being on the street was not safe. Luckily, most people were in the Katharsis Dome, or they would have run the risk of being recognized. They needed to find somewhere safe, and then find a way to disguise themselves.

Qui-Gon raised his hood. It would conceal his face somewhat. "It's getting chilly," he remarked.

"We're almost there," Den replied.

He led them a few blocks on. A tall gray tower was surrounded by a high polished gate of bronze metal.

"Well, here we are. Do you have an appointment?" Den asked. "They won't let you in without an ID tag. It's top security."

Qui-Gon eyed the sleek façade of the building. There were no windows and there appeared to be only one entrance. Once they got in, they would have to get out the same way.

"Our appointment is for tomorrow," he said. "We just wanted to see where it was."

"Do you have a place to stay tonight?" Den asked. "I live in a place where you can rent guest rooms. It's close to here."

Qui-Gon hesitated. It had not slipped his notice that Den seemed to appear whenever they needed help. He did not sense danger from him, but he was still wary.

But an uneasiness that had nothing to do with Den had been ticking away inside him. Obi-Wan was now a wanted criminal. They had barely been on Telos an hour, and already the situation had escalated out of control. Qui-Gon had felt sure back on Coruscant that if events got out of hand, he would be able to order Obi-Wan back to the Temple. Now the boy was trapped on the planet. He would not be able to pass through security in order to leave.

He had brought the boy into danger. He had done it with his eyes open. Guilt pierced him. He had to protect Obi-Wan now. He could not let his passion for bringing Xanatos to justice interfere with the boy's safety.

"Well, come along and have a look, at least," Den urged in a friendly way. "I'm only a few blocks away."

Qui-Gon nodded. He could see that Obi-Wan looked tired, and suddenly reflected that the boy had not eaten a bite since breakfast. Obi-Wan needed rest and food. He could find that for him at least.

He would trust his instincts. Den might be a gambler, but he didn't seem like such a bad character.

Den turned off the main road and led them down an alley that twisted behind the tall buildings. The structures grew more modest as they entered a residential area. Den led them to a shabby building painted in various shades of green, blue, and red.

"My landlady is paying me to paint the place, but she can't decide on a color," he explained with a grin.

He opened the door and ushered them into a small anteroom. "Riva?" he called toward the back of the house. "I brought guests. *Paying* guests." He leaned in closer to them. "That will bring her on the run."

As if on cue, Qui-Gon heard the soft sound of running feet.

Den grinned broadly. "See what I mean?"

"That's coming from outside." Qui-Gon strode to the window and moved the curtain a fraction to look at the street outside.

Security police were racing silently down the street. An officer signaled for them to surround the building.

Qui-Gon's hand fell onto the hilt of his lightsaber. His instincts had been off. Den had betrayed them. He had led them into a trap.

CHAPTER 5

As soon as Obi-Wan saw Qui-Gon reach for his lightsaber, he activated his own. The two weapons glowed pale blue and green in the dim light of the room.

Den stumbled backward. "Jedi! Whoa! I mean, I knew you were *weird*, but I didn't know you were Jedi."

"You betrayed us for the reward," Qui-Gon said.

"Who, me?" Den asked, holding a hand over his heart. "Joke, right? Kill me now, because I'm mortally wounded. I wouldn't betray a fellow criminal. Sure, I saw that alert. But I wouldn't turn you in."

"A fellow *what*?" Obi-Wan asked.

Den peered out the curtain. "Those security police could be here for me. I thought they were looking for me in the Katharsis Dome, too. Not that I'm a criminal, exactly. I'm more like a . . . facilitator."

"And why should we believe you?" Obi-Wan asked.

"Um, let's review. Because you're a criminal, too?" Den stepped back from the curtain. "You can put away those saber things. I've got a way out."

Obi-Wan exchanged a glance with Qui-Gon. Qui-Gon shrugged. What else could they do? Better to trust Den a little longer than to tangle with twenty security officers.

Den led them down the hallway to the kitchen. He hurried to a panel in the wall and pushed it open. "After you," he said to Obi-Wan.

A foul smell rose in Obi-Wan's nostrils. "The garbage chute?"

"Do you have a better idea?" Den asked. "Okay, if you insist, I'll go first."

He swung himself into the small space and then let go. They heard the sound of banging and a small *ow!* Then Den's voice came to them hollowly.

"Uh, not that I want to tell two Jedi what to do, but you might want to speed it up."

Obi-Wan swung into the chute and let go. He bumped down past the remnants of rotten vegetables and food. His hand slid in something slimy, and then he tumbled out onto a large bin full of garbage. A moment later, Qui-Gon slid out next to him.

"That was a treat," Qui-Gon said, picking a rotten leaf off his tunic. "Thanks."

"My pleasure. This way," Den urged.

They climbed out of the garbage bin and followed Den through a hallway that was lined with shelves crammed with food tins. "Fifty years ago Telos had a famine," Den explained. "My landlady was only ten at the time, but she never forgot it. She's crazier than I am."

At last the dark hallway ended at a slanted door. "This will bring us up into the gardens," Den explained in a whisper. "It doesn't look as though it belongs to the house, so ten to one they won't have it surrounded."

"Ten to one?" Qui-Gon asked.

"Good odds!" Den assured him. "Look, you still don't trust me? Kill me now. Go ahead. Put me out of my misery. Run me through with that glowy tube thing if I'm wrong. No? Okay, come on."

Qui-Gon shot an amused look at Obi-Wan, which Obi-Wan answered with a frown. He didn't know why Qui-Gon always seemed to give his trust to the scoundrels they met. Yet when it came to Obi-Wan, Qui-Gon was strict and unbending.

Den eased open the slanted door overhead. They climbed up a short flight of stairs and slipped outside. They were surrounded by tall rows of a green-leafed plant.

Den jerked his head to indicate which way they should go. They could hear the security police kicking in the doors of the rooming house as they quickly made their way through the rustling plants, trying not to stir the leaves any more than the wind did.

When they reached the end of the field, Den hesitated.

"What do we do now?" Obi-Wan asked.

Suddenly, blaster fire ripped into the row of plants to their right.

"Um, let me think. Run?" Den suggested.

They took off, zigzagging through the remaining fields. Qui-Gon glanced back and saw the security police giving chase.

"We have a good lead," Den shouted. "We can outrun them. At least they're not on speeder bikes."

Just then, three speeder bikes took off after them.

"Oops," Den panted.

"Activate your lightsaber!" Qui-Gon called to Obi-Wan.

They did not slow their pace, keeping up with

Den. The Force told them when to turn back and deflect the fire with their lightsabers.

Den zigzagged down a maze of alleys. The speeder bikes gained on them.

"Just hang on, almost there," he called back.

They came to a field with a drainage pipe rising out of the grass. Den flattened himself and crawled in. Quickly, Obi-Wan and Qui-Gon followed. The speeder bike engines buzzed angrily overhead. Blaster fire peppered the pipe but did not penetrate the metal.

"This goes underground and leads into a basement nearby," Den said. "They'll never find us."

"You said that before," Obi-Wan grunted.

"I said ten-to-one," Den corrected. "I'll give you better odds this time."

On their hands and knees, they crawled through rusty water with a skin of muck on top.

"Den, what used to drain through this pipe?" Qui-Gon asked. The smell was worse than the garbage chute.

"Don't ask," Den said cheerfully.

At last they saw a faint beam of light. They spilled out onto a basement floor, their tunics stained with rust, garbage, and a substance Obi-Wan did not want to identify.

Den led them upstairs and out a side door

into an alley. He looked both ways, then overhead. "You see? Saved."

"Will you be safe from here?" Qui-Gon asked.

"Joke, right? You can't leave me now!" Den protested. "I'm not finished saving your necks yet. Come on, I led you into trouble. Let me lead you out again. I have a safe place for you to stay."

"Safe like the last place?" Obi-Wan asked.

"This place is different," Den assured them. "It's a hideout of a friend of mine. Look, the security police will be everywhere. You need to lay low, even for a few hours."

"And why should we trust you?" Qui-Gon asked.

"Because you have no choice?" Den said.

"One always has a choice," Qui-Gon said. "But we'll follow."

CHAPTER 6

Obi-Wan couldn't believe it. Den was obviously a criminal. Why was Qui-Gon trusting him with their lives?

When Den walked ahead, he posed the same question to Qui-Gon. The Jedi only sighed.

"Think about it, Obi-Wan. We are criminals, too, at least in the eyes of the security police. Who can hide us better than those who are already in hiding?"

Qui-Gon put his hand on Obi-Wan's shoulder. "Don't worry. The core of him is pure."

"Kill me now, because I can't feel it," Obi-Wan grumbled. Still he liked the comforting hand on his shoulder. It almost felt as though Qui-Gon and he were Master and apprentice again.

Den led them to another part of the city, well off the wide boulevards of the city's center. Here the buildings huddled together as if a cold wind had driven them closer for warmth and protection.

Den led them to a building in the middle of the block. Instead of entering, he slipped down an alley. A broken pipe hung down the side of the building, swinging free. Den pulled himself up and straddled it.

"It's easier than it looks," he said. He grinned at the exasperated expression on Obi-Wan's face. "Hey, kid. You've gone down a garbage chute and climbed through a drainpipe. I think you can do this."

With an irritated glance at Qui-Gon, Obi-Wan grabbed the pipe. From the street it had looked ready to fall on the first unsuspecting head, but he found that it was actually anchored firmly to the wall. There were small metal bolts screwed in the sides, undetectable from below but big enough to serve as handholds and footholds. Den was right — it was easier to climb than it looked.

Obi-Wan hoisted himself up and over the edge of the flat roof. A water tank rose in a corner, a rusting spiral staircase circling it up to a platform at the top.

"Don't tell me," Obi-Wan said. "We're going to jump in that water tank next."

"Joke!" Den said, chuckling. He crossed to the tank and knocked a rhythmic series of taps against it. A short rap answered him.

"She's in," he said. "Let's go."

Obi-Wan followed Den up the spiral staircase to the top of the tank. When he reached the platform, he saw that the ceiling was recessed. It was painted to look like dark water. Anyone from above would not be able to tell that this water tower was any different from the others that dotted the roofs nearby.

Den slid open a trap door and disappeared inside. Obi-Wan followed.

To his relief, he found himself on a staircase leading down into a cozy apartment. The walls were round and made of durasteel. A thick rug was on the floor, and there were comfortable places to sit. In the center of the space was a long table piled with tech equipment.

A slender young woman rose from her seat at the table. Her hair was dark chestnut, wound in several braids around her head. Her eyes were a warm honey-brown. Right now they were trained suspiciously on Qui-Gon and Obi-Wan.

"Who have you brought me this time, Den?" she asked.

"Friends," Den responded.

"They're always friends," she said warily. Her eyes flicked over their stained tunics. "And they're dressed so nicely, too."

"We had a little trouble getting here. But they might be able to help us." He turned to Qui-Gon and Obi-Wan. "This is Andra. She's the head of the POWER party — Preserve Our Wild Endangered Resources. Andra, this is Qui-Gon Jinn and Obi-Wan Kenobi, two Jedi visitors who seem to be wanted by the security police."

Her eyes narrowed. "Wanted? For what?"

Den took a piece of fruit from a bowl and tossed it to Obi-Wan. "Here, kid, you look hungry. What does it matter what they're wanted for, Andra? We need them. They want to know about UniFy."

Andra's suspicion changed to interest. She looked at them curiously.

"Maybe you could explain what it is you do," Qui-Gon suggested. "What is the POWER party?"

"We are a political party in opposition to those in control of the government," she answered. "Unfortunately, we're illegal right now. The government outlawed us. We were the first to raise the cry when the government gave the stewardship of our sacred places to UniFy. We asked why our land was turned over to private interests, why we were forced to trust the word of a corporation that they would preserve and protect the land. Most didn't listen. They were happy to have the tax burden taken away. But some did listen, and joined us. We're made up of former government officials, scientists, environmental workers, ordinary citizens who listened back when we were allowed to speak. Now we've gone into hiding and meet here when we can."

"Do you have proof that UniFy is mishandling your sacred spaces?" Qui-Gon asked.

She hesitated. "We had evidence that something is going on at the Sacred Pools. Three people went to the global park to gather images and evidence. They were killed in a speeder accident on the way back to Thani. They told me that they had hard evidence of something, but they didn't say what it was. I think their death was no accident. The evidence they were bringing back was destroyed. We are mobilizing to make another trip." She pushed impatiently at a stray hair that had escaped a braid. "It's difficult. Security is very tight at the global parks. They say they need to keep people away until the land is reclaimed. We think they are exploiting it, mapping it for further development."

"Why don't the people of Telos ask more questions about what is being done?" Qui-Gon asked. "This world is known for the conservation of its natural beauties. Even from an economic standpoint, it doesn't make sense. Tourism is a large industry here."

Andra looked bleak. "Katharsis. The people are obsessed with betting on it, with hoping they'll be chosen in the lottery. And they don't worry about the tourists — more come for Katharsis now than the global parks. Greed has entered the people like a fever." She gave Qui-Gon a cool questioning look. "So why do you think you can help?"

"I don't," Qui-Gon said bluntly. "That was Den's idea."

"You seem very interested in UniFy," Den said. "This is only a guess, but I have a feeling that you don't have an appointment tomorrow."

Qui-Gon said nothing. Obi-Wan admired his reserve. He was able to convey patience and a willingness to listen without giving anything away.

"So are you an environmentalist like Andra?" Obi-Wan asked Den.

Before he could answer, Andra laughed. "You mean have a commitment to something bigger than himself? Not Den. Our arrangement is strictly for credits."

"Hey, wait a second," Den said huffily. "I have just as many ideals as the next guy."

"If the next guy happens to be a smuggler or a thief," Andra shot back. She turned back to Obi-Wan and Qui-Gon. "When we first went underground, we needed tech equipment. I had to forage for computer parts and comlinks on the black market. That's how I met Den. He's been smuggling the parts we need to keep going. We've managed to get out an underground paper alerting the people to what we think is happening. But Den's allegiance is only to the credits I can give him."

"Excuse me for needing money to live, Captain Integrity," Den said to Andra. "Not everyone can live on ideals. Especially when they don't pay rent. If it weren't for me, you'd be talking to these walls instead of the 'people' out there."

"How like you to claim our success as your own," Andra said coolly.

"See what you get when you try to help people?" Den grumbled to the Jedi. "Insults. No wonder I'm a thief."

Andra ignored him and turned back to Qui-Gon and Obi-Wan. "You can stay here if you like. Any enemy of UniFy is a friend of mine."

"I didn't say I was an enemy of UniFy," Qui-Gon said with a smile.

She studied him for a moment. "But you are, aren't you? Maybe Den is right. Maybe we can help each other. But you have to tell me why you're here. Not to mention why you're wanted by the security police."

"I'm not sure what the charge is, but I'm sure it's serious," Qui-Gon admitted. "It's false, whatever it is. We have a powerful enemy on

Telos. I believe he is using UniFy as a shell corporation for his own company."

"Which is?" Andra asked.

"Offworld."

Andra let out a long breath. "Offworld . . . They are the largest mining concern in the galaxy." Two spots of color appeared on her cheeks. "But that means that UniFy could be mapping our lands for mining development! If we could prove the two companies are linked, we'd have proof of UniFy's plans!"

"Andra hired me to break into the UniFy files," Den told them. "I worked there a few months ago, and I forgot to turn in my ID badge. I had to leave in a hurry."

"You forgot?" Qui-Gon asked.

Den grinned. "And then I mistakenly took a couple extra badges when I left. So I can get us in. The odds are totally in our favor."

Qui-Gon hesitated. He turned to Andra. "You don't seem to trust him. Why should we?"

"Because I won't let you down!" Den cried.

"I did not ask you the question," Qui-Gon said sternly.

Andra sighed. "What's in it for you, Den? Why would you take the risk of breaking in again?"

"Because I didn't finish the job you paid me for," Den told her. "I feel badly about that. I have my integrity, you know."

"You're a thief!" Andra cried in exasperation.

"Exactly!" Den exclaimed. "So let me steal!"

"Why don't I feel reassured?" Obi-Wan wondered aloud.

Andra sighed. "I know exactly what you mean."

CHAPTER 7

Besides the identity cards, Den had managed to steal the gray unisuits that the lowest level of tech workers at UniFy wore. It was surprisingly easy to join the stream of workers entering the building at dawn the next day. The security guards swiped their cards and they simply walked through.

Sure, we're in, Obi-Wan thought. *But will it be as easy to get out again?* For some reason, Qui-Gon had decided to trust this Den character. And the Jedi Council thought *he* was too impulsive.

Den took the turbolift down to a lower level. "The main files are in a restricted area," he explained. "We'll have to walk down the utility staircase. Then there's a guard at the door. Can you wave those lightsabers of yours at him? We can lock him in a closet until we're done."

"Just leave it to me," Qui-Gon said.

They slipped down the utility staircase and entered a long white hallway lit with soothing glow lights. A security guard sat in front of a console at the end.

"Passes," he said shortly.

Qui-Gon handed him his identity card. He focused on the Telosian's mind. "This will do. Go on in."

"This will do," the guard said. "Go on in."

The door hissed open, and they walked through.

"What was that?" Den asked wonderingly.

"A Jedi tool," Qui-Gon answered. "The Force can easily be used on the weak-minded."

"I am impressed," Den said, shaking his head in admiration. "Can you imagine what you could do with that, if you had a little larceny in you? Hey, do you think your Jedi Temple would take a guy like me?"

"No," Qui-Gon said shortly, accessing the door marked SECURE FILES.

The room was filled with computers and holographic files. Den crossed immediately to the main terminal.

"I'll break into the system, and the two of you can search on the other monitors," he said, his fingers flying over the keys. "They changed the password, but I wrote a program that . . . there we go! Call me a genius and I won't argue with you."

Qui-Gon sat at another terminal and motioned Obi-Wan to the next. It would be faster if they all searched independently.

Files names and numbers flashed onscreen. There were many marked SACRED POOLS. "There are at least three hundred files here," Qui-Gon said after a moment. "Let's break it down. Den, you take the first hundred, Obi-Wan the next. I'll do the last. Scan as quickly as you can. Look for any mention of Offworld, mining, or mapping." He looked over at Den. "Don't try anything."

Den blinked at him innocently. "Like what?"

"I don't want to speculate," Qui-Gon said dryly. "Just do what I say."

Obi-Wan accessed the first file and quickly scanned it. It was a record of correspondence between the manager of the Sacred Pools project and his superior at UniFy. As far as he could see, it was reporting fuel and food needs for the workers. Nothing. He accessed the next.

And the next. And the next . . . Obi-Wan waded through file after file. He never imagined that working for a large corporation could be so dull. Information was repeated over and over and double-checked. He saw nothing suspicious.

"I wish Tahl were here," Qui-Gon muttered. "She would be able to figure out these financial records. They make everything so complicated . . ."

Suddenly, Qui-Gon stopped talking. Obi-Wan noticed that his viewscreen had frozen. When he looked back at his own, he saw that it was frozen as well.

"Den, what's happening?" he asked.

"I don't know," Den said worriedly. He tried to turn his viewscreen off, but the switch didn't work. "Odds are it's a temporary glitch." He sprang up from his chair and started toward the door. "Just lay low."

"Where are you going?" Qui-Gon asked.

"I'm just going to nose around, see what's going on. You can rely on me."

Den slipped out the door. Qui-Gon slowly rose.

"We have to get out of here now," he said.

Obi-Wan looked at him, surprised. "But we can't abandon Den."

Qui-Gon looked grim. "He has already abandoned us."

Obi-Wan heard the sound of pounding feet. The door hissed open.

"Don't draw your lightsaber," Qui-Gon quickly ordered, just before the security forces rushed in.

Obi-Wan knew why. Qui-Gon was hoping to escape detection as a wanted criminal. If they were lucky, they would be held at UniFy as trespassers.

But that fleeting hope was dashed immediately when the burly head of security stepped forward.

"You are wanted as violators of Telosian law under the Galactic Criminals Act," he told them. "You are under arrest."

CHAPTER 8

Obi-Wan and Qui-Gon were swiftly transported to the Central Booking Station, where they were recognized as escaped galactic criminals and thrown into prison. Qui-Gon asked that the Temple be contacted, but the request was ignored.

"Telosian justice used to be fair," he said to Obi-Wan as he stood in the dank underground cell. "They should allow us the opportunity to clear ourselves."

"We're not even sure what the charges are," Obi-Wan said. "Do you think they'll discover that the whole thing has been faked?"

"There is always that hope," Qui-Gon said. "They can't hold us for long if they can't prove we did something wrong. At least they didn't find our lightsabers."

Using the Force, Qui-Gon had managed to

prevent the guards from giving them a thorough search.

"Why don't we just cut through the door?" Obi-Wan asked, placing his hands against the fortified durasteel.

"Because there will be fifty guards on us before we can move very far," Qui-Gon said. "Let's bide our time. We'll find an opportunity to escape."

"I can't believe Den left us in the lurch like that," Obi-Wan said, disgusted. "He must have known there was a security alert as soon as the viewscreens froze."

"Yes, I think he did," Qui-Gon agreed calmly. "But it is better to focus on what we can do now."

"What can we do?" Obi-Wan asked. "We're locked up."

"We can think of our next step," Qui-Gon said. "It's a waste of time to blame Den. What did we learn while we were at UniFy?"

"I didn't learn anything except that people who work for companies send too many memos," Obi-Wan said, discouraged.

"There were many, it's true," Qui-Gon agreed. "And most of them were trivial. Many of them merely confirmed a conversation over a comlink. Did you notice that? This makes me think that so many files could be a way to stop examiners later should the company be investigated. It's hard to find the truth when it's buried under data. Does that remind you of anything?"

Obi-Wan thought for a long moment. "Offworld," he said at last. "The company conceals its true intentions and even its headquarters behind other companies. It uses confusion to hide."

"Exactly," Qui-Gon said. "And there was something else I learned at UniFy. When the screens froze, I got to see what Den was doing. He was not looking up files on Offworld or the Sacred Pools. He was looking up Katharsis."

"Why?" Obi-Wan asked.

"I don't know the answer to that, but the question is interesting," Qui-Gon said. "UniFy administers the funds from the lottery, so I suppose it should have Katharsis files. But why is Den so interested? Think about his character."

Obi-Wan remembered Andra's words. "He must think he can profit in some way."

"Exactly," Qui-Gon agreed. "My guess is that's the reason he agreed to help us in the first place. So you see when we get out, we'll have another path to investigate."

"When we get out?" Obi-Wan asked, looking at the fortified durasteel door.

"We'll get out," Qui-Gon said in the same calm tone.

Obi-Wan wished he could feel as certain. He had a feeling that now that Xanatos had them where he wanted them, he would not be so foolish as to let them go.

They spent a cold night in the cell. Obi-Wan awoke before dawn. He lay on a sleep mat, his eyes open. There were no windows in the cell, so he could not distinguish the walls from the floor. He was surrounded by black, as though he were floating in a void. Perhaps this disorienting feeling was part of the punishment.

The only indication of morning was when the cell lights blazed on. They were given some hard bread and weak tea for breakfast.

The day passed slowly. Qui-Gon asked repeatedly to speak to someone in authority. The request was refused.

Qui-Gon and Obi-Wan did a series of muscle stretches to stay limber. Then they meditated. In captivity, a Jedi organized the mind, calmed the spirit, and kept the body strong.

Qui-Gon sat meditating on the hard stone floor. Suddenly, he sighed and raised his head.

"I'm sorry, Obi-Wan."

Obi-Wan was surprised by this statement. "Sorry?" he asked.

"You should be back at the Temple. I should

not have let you accompany me. It was an error in judgment."

"The decision was mine to make," Obi-Wan said. "I'm not sorry to be here."

Qui-Gon's smile was as dim as the light. "Even though you are cold and hungry?"

"I am where I should be," Obi-Wan responded. "By your side."

Qui-Gon stood. "I was harsh to you after what happened on Melida/Daan."

"No more than I deserved." Obi-Wan was surprised to see the emotion on Qui-Gon's face. This was the first time his former Master had brought up the rift between them with sorrow more than anger. He seemed to be struggling for words.

"No, Obi-Wan, it was much more than you deserved," Qui-Gon corrected. "I have come to see that my reaction was due to my own failings, not yours. I haven't had a chance to tell you that. I —" Qui-Gon stopped suddenly. "He's here," he murmured.

Then Obi-Wan felt it, too. The disturbance in the Force was like a whisper of poison gas that snaked under a crack in the door and then filled the room. He stood and turned toward the door.

The durasteel door suddenly hissed open. Xanatos stood in the doorway. His black cloak was thrown back, his legs casually apart, his hands on his hips.

"Enjoying yourselves?" he asked, cocking an eyebrow at them and smiling.

Qui-Gon faced him, not speaking.

"Ah, the silent treatment," Xanatos said with a sigh. "And here I was hoping that we could have a chat. There's not much time. Your punishment has been decided."

"But we didn't have a trial," Qui-Gon said quietly.

"Oh, but you did," Xanatos answered. "You were both considered too dangerous to attend."

"We have the right to attend our own trial! That isn't fair!" Obi-Wan exclaimed.

Xanatos shook his head. "Ah, I remember being that young. Back when I thought that life would treat me fairly. Before I met you, Qui-Gon Jinn."

"Life does not treat you fairly or unfairly," Qui-Gon said. "It merely is. It is up to each of us to be fair, or unfair."

"It's never too late for some great Jedi wisdom," Xanatos said scornfully. "And it is always the same — nothing but riddles. Well, figure this out, Jedi — since you did not appear at your trial, I showed up in your place. I was the star witness against you. I had evidence of your crimes, records of the many worlds that brought charges against you, tales of the times you had escaped justice throughout the galaxy. And at last justice found you on Telos. It also helped that a grieving father was in the courtroom, distraught at the death of his son at the hands of your accomplice." Xanatos gave a heavy sigh. "Poor Bruck. I always thought he just needed a little push to succeed. How was I to know that Obi-Wan Kenobi would deliver it?"

Xanatos raised one hand and then slapped it into his palm with a sharp *crack*. It was eerily close to the crack of Bruck's head hitting the rocks below the waterfall. Obi-Wan tried not to wince. He would not give Xanatos that satisfaction. But inside, he felt the shock of it. Helplessness and guilt swept over him as he recalled Bruck's lifeless, unseeing gaze, the arm flung out as if in a last, desperate cry for help.

"The court may have listened to your lies," Qui-Gon said quickly, sensing Obi-Wan's distress and trying to deflect Xanatos. "But when the Temple learns —"

Xanatos laughed. "By the time the Temple learns of your fate, you will already be dead. That is your punishment, Jedi. You have been sentenced to death."

Suddenly Xanatos leaned forward. His blue eyes burned like the hottest part of a flame. His pale skin seemed to tighten over his bones. His face looked like a skull with eyes of fire.

"And I will be there to watch you die," he hissed in Qui-Gon's face.

CHAPTER 9

They did not get a chance to say another word, or call for help. Xanatos made sure that an entire troop of guards surrounded them. They were led through the prison corridors to the courtyard in front.

The sun was low in the sky. The two adjacent prison towers cast two long ominous shadows across the courtyard. A crowd filled the yard and spilled out into the street. When they saw the prisoners, they erupted in catcalls and jeers.

"They love the executions," one of the guards murmured to the other.

Qui-Gon felt a sinister energy emanating from the crowd. Telos had never had public executions. Such displays were limited to more primitive worlds. What had happened to peaceful Telos? It only took one man to corrupt it, if that man was as sly and powerful as Xanatos.

Qui-Gon felt reassured by the presence of his

lightsaber underneath his cloak. Still, he did not know when he would get a chance to use it.

A scaffold slowly rose on repulsorlifts until it floated high above the crowd. Two burly guards stood next to two durasteel hinged slabs. A chute ran from the slabs to the edge of the platform. Vibro-axes were leaning against the slabs. Qui-Gon saw in an instant how the execution would take place. He and Obi-Wan would be forced to lie on the slabs. They would be beheaded by the vibro-axes, the hinges would drop, and their heads would roll down the chute and come to rest facing the crowd.

It was gruesome, but quick.

Qui-Gon saw Obi-Wan swallow. For the first time, he was seriously worried. He had thought that at any moment an opportunity would come for them to escape. But how could they make their way through the crowd? Even if they could deal with the guards and Xanatos, the crowd would rise against them.

They were placed in an energy cage that was hoisted up above the mass of people. The angry crowd shouted for their deaths to be painful and slow. Xanatos stood at the top of the stairs, watching the cage rise with avid eyes.

It was the duty of every Jedi to accept death when it came. Yet Qui-Gon could not be calm. It was not his time. It was not Obi-Wan's. He saw that Obi-Wan was struggling to contain his fear.

"Kill them! Kill the murderers!" the crowd shouted.

Anger surged in Qui-Gon. Xanatos had done this. He had inflamed the crowd. He had filled their minds with hatred and lies. If Qui-Gon died, Xanatos would win. He would corrupt Telos even more. He would destroy it.

Qui-Gon couldn't let that happen.

Yet he must not fight with anger. He must fight with justice.

"We must not give up," Qui-Gon told Obi-Wan urgently over the noise of the crowd. "They will need to retract the energy bars for the executioners to get us on those slabs. That's when we will fight. All is not lost. Stay calm and alert."

Obi-Wan nodded.

Qui-Gon noted the steady resolution in Obi-Wan's eyes. They had little chance of escaping this fate, but Obi-Wan accepted this. The boy was never cowed by odds against him.

The energy cage slowly lowered toward the scaffold. Security police on swoops hovered near in case the prisoners tried to escape.

The cries of the crowd came to Qui-Gon faintly. All his attention was now focused on the guards on the scaffold. He was confident that he and Obi-Wan could take them. But what then? They would have to leap to the ground, even as blaster fire pounded them from above and below. Perhaps the surprise of their move would increase the likelihood of escape. Perhaps the crowd was not as bloodthirsty as it appeared. But he did not like these odds. Even Den would not take this bet, Qui-Gon thought ruefully.

The guards on the scaffold walked forward. Qui-Gon waited for the energy bars to lower. As soon as they did, he would spring forward.

Out of the corner of his eye, he noted an erratic movement from one of the swoops. He looked to the side without turning his head. The rider was hooded. In only the split second he allowed himself to glance, Qui-Gon recognized who it was. The surprise hit him broadside. Andra.

"Behind you, Obi-Wan," he said in a low voice. "Be prepared."

The energy bars retracted. The guards rushed forward. Qui-Gon and Obi-Wan activated their lightsabers simultaneously and leaped toward them. Blaster fire pinged around them, and they deflected it, swinging in a blur of motion faster than the eye could follow.

Another swoop joined Andra. The two crafts dived toward them, engines screaming.

"Jump!" he called to Obi-Wan. He leaped off

the scaffold as the swoop dived to scoop him up. The other vehicle did the same for Obi-Wan. Qui-Gon caught a quick flash of a determined Den.

Qui-Gon landed on his feet. He held on to the driver's shoulders and lowered himself into the seat as the swoop dived, turned, climbed, hovered, and turned again, trying to evade the guards giving chase.

Qui-Gon still had his lightsaber in his hand. He deflected blaster fire as the craft darted around the guards. He saw Obi-Wan doing the same. It was hard to keep his balance on the agile swoop, but he managed.

In a daring move, the swoops headed straight for the prison towers. Qui-Gon saw the towers grow closer and closer, so close he could see the cracks and pits in the surface. At the very last moment, Andra turned sharply. They came so close that Qui-Gon's hand was scraped. Two of the swoops pursuing them crashed into the towers. Andra and Den zoomed away.

Qui-Gon allowed himself one glance back. The last thing he saw was Xanatos, standing straight and tall and unmoving, watching him go. He could feel the coiled hatred spring at him from across the distance. They would meet again, he knew. Xanatos would make sure of it.

CHAPTER 10

When she was sure they were away from their pursuers, Andra loosened her hood.

"Thanks for not falling off," she called back to Qui-Gon.

"Thanks for rescuing us," Qui-Gon responded. "I was almost starting to worry."

She grinned and gunned the motor. In another few minutes, they landed in the alley near her house. Den and Andra concealed the swoops behind a pile of rusty abandoned floaters.

"Whoa!" Den called as he swept off his hood. "Did we beat those odds, or what? The next time I'm outrunning some security police, I want a Jedi at my back!"

Obi-Wan didn't respond to Den's friendly grin. "You wouldn't have had to rescue us if you'd warned us back at UniFy," he pointed out.

"I was about to," Den protested. "I didn't get the chance. At least I came through in the end."

"Only because I insisted," Andra said. "I'm the one who proposed the rescue."

"Kill me now if I wasn't going to! You didn't give me a chance!" Den protested.

"I suggest we continue this inside," Qui-Gon said, his eyes sweeping the sky overhead with a glance. "In my experience, security on Telos doesn't give up easily."

They climbed up the drain and entered Andra's snug home. Andra began to heat some drinks and set out a plate of bread and fruit. Obi-Wan reached for it hungrily.

"I don't know what to do now," Andra said worriedly. "We can't break into UniFy again. I'm sure they plugged the holes in their security. We'll never be able to get the proof we need that UniFy is tied to Offworld."

"If only we'd had more time to look," Den said.

Qui-Gon gave him a hard look. "But you weren't looking very hard for an Offworld connection, were you?"

Den shifted in his seat. "Of course I was. There were too many files. You said so yourself."

"I saw your screen, Den," Qui-Gon said. "You weren't looking at the Sacred Pool files. You were looking up Katharsis."

"Katharsis?" Andra turned. "Why?"

"Don't look at me like that, all of you," Den protested. "I'm an honest man!"

Qui-Gon cocked an eyebrow. Obi-Wan looked disgusted. Andra blew out an exasperated breath.

"Okay, so I'm not one hundred percent honest," Den admitted. "But I'm loyal! I *was* looking up Katharsis. When I worked there I found out by chance — well, not so much by chance, but because I broke into some files — that UniFy controls Katharsis."

Andra swiveled, the pot in her hand. "You mean the government doesn't control it?"

Den nodded. "They just want you to think they do. If everyone knew that a corporation controlled Katharsis, they'd realize that . . ."

"UniFy decides how the profits from Katharsis are spent," Andra said rapidly. "Which means they totally control our public lands."

Den nodded. "UniFy came up with the idea for Katharsis in the first place. They paid off some key government people in order to push it through. Basically, the government is in UniFy's pocket."

Andra sank into a chair, stunned. "Do you think that UniFy deliberately devised Katharsis just to distract the population from their intentions? They're going to open all our global parks for development. And we're going to pay for it!"

"It's pretty diabolical," Den said. "You almost have to admire it. Some kind of evil genius had to come up with this plan."

Qui-Gon exchanged a glance with Obi-Wan. "Xanatos," he said quietly. The plan had a simple elegance to its evil that was pure Xanatos.

But Qui-Gon wasn't finished with Den. "Why were you looking up Katharsis again, Den?" he asked. "If you knew this already, there wasn't much more to discover."

They all turned to Den. He met their gaze with steady innocence. That meant he was no doubt about to lie, Qui-Gon guessed.

"I was just hoping to help Andra and the POWER party —" he started.

Andra interrupted him. "Don't con me, Den. Not now. This is too important."

He looked at her a long moment. Qui-Gon noticed the vulnerability in the look. *He cares for her,* he realized.

"Okay," he said. "I *was* hoping to help you. But I was also looking for a way to rig the lottery."

"Always looking out for yourself, aren't you?" Andra said bitterly.

"No," Den said quietly. "I look out for you, too. But you won't see that."

"So did you find out how to rig it?" Qui-Gon asked.

"Not exactly," Den hedged.

"Did you find out anything?" Obi-Wan asked impatiently.

"Yes, I found out something," Den admitted. "The lottery already *is* rigged."

CHAPTER 11

"Things are happening too fast here," Andra said weakly. "Let me pour the tea."

They sat around the table, warm mugs of tea in their hands. The enormity of the plan stunned Andra. She had expected conspiracies and corruption, but not on such a vast scale. It was obvious that they had stumbled on a scheme to take over the resources of an entire planet. The question was how the pieces fit together, and what they could do about it.

Qui-Gon drained his mug. "I suggest a two-part plan," he said. "First, Den will infiltrate the lottery system."

"Whoa, hold on," Den said. "What do you mean, I'll infiltrate the lottery system? What makes you think I can do that?"

"I have a feeling you already know how," Qui-Gon said coolly. "Why else would you risk so much to get back inside UniFy? Why else did the security get triggered? You were able to in-vade the system."

Den took a gulp of tea, then coughed. No one moved to help him.

"Okay, okay," he croaked. "I think I can rig it. I mean, I think I can rig the part that's already rigged."

"And you know how to ensure that you'll win the prize," Qui-Gon said.

Den nodded reluctantly. "I can rig it so that I win the lottery. One winner is always someone selected by UniFy in advance. As the games go on, some contestants are given faulty equip-ment — not anything they would notice, but something slightly off that decreases their chances of winning. One of the contestants has been selected in advance and bribed. He or she agrees to pass half the fortune back under the table to the company. I can just put my name in the next winner's place."

Andra shook her head. "I knew you had an ul-terior motive to helping me. You were going to take that fortune and run."

"Joke, right?" Den said. "Because I can't be-lieve you would really think such a thing. After I won my fortune, I would have shared it. Some of it."

"I don't want any part of a fortune built on destroying our sacred spaces," Andra said fiercely. "And you shouldn't either!"

"It's not my fault they're being exploited!" Den protested. "And a fortune is a fortune."

"That's your trouble," Andra said. "You really believe that."

"Does anyone want to hear the second part of my plan?" Qui-Gon interrupted mildly. "Second, we should follow through on Andra's original plan to visit the Sacred Pools. We'll need to gather the evidence all over again."

"It won't be easy," Andra said. "The security is extremely tight."

"Just use some of that Jedi mind-altering-voice-bending stuff," Den suggested.

"I'm afraid we'll need more than that," Qui-Gon said. "Andra, can you call in your supporters? I think the best plan is to infiltrate at several points so that we don't rely on only one team."

Andra looked down at her mug. She smoothed the wood of the table with her hand.

"Andra?" Qui-Gon prodded.

She looked up. "I can't do that," she said. "I haven't been completely honest with you all. I have no supporters. I *am* the POWER party."

"There's no party?" Obi-Wan asked in disbelief.

She shrugged and gave a small smile. "Just me. I had a few supporters, but they all fell away when the investigative team was killed. No one will listen to me anymore. They all think I'm crazy because I see a bleak future no one wants to face, let alone prevent."

Suddenly, Den burst out laughing. "So Captain Integrity has been lying all along!" he chortled. "This is the best news I've heard in a millennium!"

"Knock it off, Den," Andra growled. "I had to pretend to have support. I needed you to help me."

"Right," Den said, nodding. "Of course. You're allowed to trick someone because you're saving the planet. I get it. As long as you have a pure motive, you can do whatever you want."

"That's not what I'm saying," Andra shot back angrily. "If you cared about anything other than yourself, you'd understand."

"I understand that you'd do anything to get what you want," Den said. "We're more alike than you want to admit, Andra."

Andra glared at him. "I'd rather be compared to a dinko."

"Sure, I can do that," Den said promptly. "A dinko is a creature with fangs and a nasty disposition. The problem is, how are you different? Let me see your teeth."

"Just keep it up, Den," Andra warned.

"Okay, enough," Qui-Gon snapped. "We

have a problem. Who's going to invade the Sacred Pools?"

"I will," Andra said, with a furious glance at Den.

"I'll go with you," Obi-Wan said.

Qui-Gon shook his head. "No."

"But it makes sense," Obi-Wan argued. "A boy traveling with a woman won't attract as much attention. We'd look like a brother and sister on an excursion. If we get caught, Andra and I can claim we got lost."

"And you should stay here and watch Den," Andra said to Qui-Gon. "If he rigs the lottery, he could take the fortune and leave the planet."

"Thanks for your support," Den said sarcastically.

"Have you given me any reason to trust you lately?" Andra asked coolly.

"Dinko," Den shot at her.

"Thief," she shot back.

Qui-Gon ignored their bickering for the moment. He felt exasperated and worried. He didn't want Obi-Wan to travel without him. Xanatos was on the loose, on his home planet, and he was enraged at their escape. But the boy's logic was sound. They had to take a risk in order to bring Xanatos down. But was this risk more than he was willing to take?

He saw Obi-Wan watching him. The boy was

wondering why he didn't want him to go. For Obi-Wan, it would be a question of trust. Qui-Gon had to allow it.

"All right," he said. "Obi-Wan and Andra will gather the evidence. Den and I will remain here. Now let's make our preparations."

CHAPTER 12

Obi-Wan and Qui-Gon stood by the swoops that would carry Obi-Wan and Andra to the Sacred Pools. Andra stood nearby with Den, checking her survival pack.

Obi-Wan had only slept for a few hours, but he felt alert and clear. A scattering of stars twinkled in the dark sky. Dawn was still an hour away. Andra felt their best chance was to invade the park in the early morning, gather pictures and evidence, and leave. They would have to be back in Thani by midday, before the end of the last round of Katharsis.

"If there is a sign of trouble, just go," Qui-Gon instructed him quietly. "If you think you cannot evade security, don't even attempt to enter the area. Survey it first."

"I've studied the maps," Obi-Wan said. "Andra knows of a way to enter without being noticed. She used it when she was a girl. She thinks it will still be there."

"Studying the map is not the same as knowing the area," Qui-Gon said. "Do not trust it completely. Make sure your entrance can be your exit."

"I know all these things," Obi-Wan said. He felt frustrated and disappointed. Qui-Gon was treating him like a fourth-year student at the Temple. He knew if Qui-Gon took him back that they would have to start over as a Master–Padawan team, but did Obi-Wan have to turn back into a child?

Qui-Gon nodded. "I know you do. It is my own unease that makes me repeat these things. I trust you, Obi-Wan."

The words trickled through Obi-Wan and filled him with warmth.

"I will not fail," he said.

"Just be safe," Qui-Gon responded.

Andra lifted her hood over her dark braids as she strode forward. "Ready, Obi-Wan?"

He swung his leg over the swoop. Qui-Gon had given him a quick lesson earlier. He wasn't used to such maneuverable transport. A slight touch could cause it to lean and dive. Obi-Wan was a fast learner, but it had taken him time before Qui-Gon was satisfied with his skill.

Andra gunned her motor and took off. Obi-Wan followed.

"Don't take any chances!" Den called after them.

"He sounds worried," Obi-Wan called over to Andra.

She gritted her teeth. "He's just trying to pretend to be a good person. It's a strain."

The black sky turned to gray as they traveled through the quiet outskirts of the city. Buildings grew farther apart. Land began to be cultivated. Then after the sun rose there were barely any dwellings at all, just occasional villages tucked into deep valleys.

Obi-Wan marveled at the beauty of the countryside. Fields of lavender and blue flowers swayed in a gentle breeze. Every few kilometers they came upon another deep blue lake glittering in the folds of the golden hills.

"This is beautiful country," he called over to Andra as they flew.

"I was born here," she said. "There's a proposal to turn much of this into another global park. But now I wonder why. Will they develop this, too?"

That reminded Obi-Wan why he was here. He hunched over the swoop handlebars, determined to foil whatever terrible scheme Xanatos had for Telos.

The land began to climb, the hills growing higher and steeper. Rock formations towered above them as they followed a road cut into the stone mountains. Snow began to appear on the crags. Although Obi-Wan had felt too warm earlier, now he was glad he had followed Andra's advice and worn his thermal gear.

"Almost there," Andra called back.

Obi-Wan followed Andra as she left the road, entering a forest glade so thick with tall trees that it blocked out the sky. Andra wove expertly through the trunks. Obi-Wan had to concentrate to keep up. At last she pulled over and waited for him to stop next to her.

"I think we should leave the swoops here," she said. "This glade adjoins the park. I know a way into the Mirror Caverns. Once we're through them, we'll be in the Park of Sacred Pools."

They covered the swoops with branches. Their footsteps made soft sounds on the carpet of leaves as they hurried through the glade. They came to a craggy wall of stone, and Andra followed it down a small hill to a fast-moving creek. She hopped from rock to rock in the creek, Obi-Wan following. The creek suddenly stopped at a sheer wall of gray stone.

"I think you can make it," Andra said, glancing back at him. "But you might have to wriggle a bit."

Obi-Wan saw that there was a slight fissure in the rock wall, almost invisible to the naked eye. It ran from the creek up the wall, as tall as he was. First, Andra pushed her survival pack through, then slipped inside. Andra was slender and was easily able to pass through, but Obi-Wan had a bit more trouble. He made himself as thin as possible and popped out, almost falling. He threw out a hand to steady himself and felt a smooth, polished surface.

Andra activated a glow rod. Obi-Wan saw that he was in a cavern with walls that arched over his head. The stone was deep black and so highly polished that he could see his reflection. Here the creek was just a trickle of silver snaking through the black floor. The beam of the glow rod bounced from wall to wall, multiplying its light. Obi-Wan felt dizzy, as though he were standing underneath a thousand stars.

"It's incredible," he said.

"Yes," Andra said quietly. "It's beautiful, isn't it? The stone is called malab. It's highly prized in the galaxy since it's so rare. Come on, the exit is this way. Watch your step, it's slippery."

She led him through twists and turns until they joined the main cave. At the entrance, the cavern widened and some light from outside illuminated the walls. Andra let out a small cry. She lifted the glow rod to examine the wall.

Stone had been chipped away, leaving deep gouges in the smooth surface. The samples were piled on the floor next to scan grids. Splinters of the stone surrounded a jagged hole in the polished floor.

"They're going to mine it," she whispered to Obi-Wan, her eyes burning. "This is a sacred place for all Telosians. Look what they've done!"

With trembling hands, she removed the holographic recorder from her pack. She trained the lens on the piles of stone, panning back and forth to the scan grids and the jagged holes. Obi-Wan took a recording rod from his pack and shot the same images. Now they would have a backup, just in case. He could conceal the recording rod in his clothing.

"Come on," Obi-Wan urged.

Carefully, they edged out of the cavern. The morning sun was strong, warming the cool rocks and lighting up golden sand that surrounded deep pools of steaming black water. A black hill rose in front of them. It glittered in the rays of the sun.

"That hill is made of malab," Andra said in disbelief. "They must be harvesting it from the caverns."

Obi-Wan looked at the heavy equipment and gravsleds surrounding the pools. He had spent time on the mining planet of Bandomeer and was familiar with mining machinery.

"Those are mole miners," he said, pointing. "They can dig hundreds of kilometers deep. If there are mole miners, there has to be a base where they unload. Those vehicles are TNTs."

"TNTs?" Andra asked.

"Treaded neutron torches," Obi-Wan explained. "They have fireball-shooting cannons that blast through rock. That's how mine shafts are created. I'd say we've got a full-scale operation going here."

He felt Andra stiffen beside him. "The pools . . ." she said. "The water used to be crystal clear."

Obi-Wan walked closer to examine a pool. As he leaned over, the cord on his survival pack dropped into the water. Steam rose in a hiss, and he pulled up the pack quickly. The cord had dissolved.

He looked up at Andra. "What happened?"

"I don't know," she said. "The pool must be contaminated. Let's look at the others."

They gathered a few long sticks and walked to the rest of the pools. When they submerged a stick in the black water, it was stripped of bark immediately. If they held it under longer, the stick itself dissolved.

"The underground spring that fed the pools

must be contaminated with chemicals," Andra said. Her voice was thick. "My father used to take me here as a girl. We hiked every inch of the park and bathed in the steam pools. After he died, this was the only place where I could find comfort."

When she looked up, Andra's honey-colored eyes glittered with unshed tears. Obi-Wan didn't know how to comfort her. What would Qui-Gon do?

He remembered an incident back at the Temple. Jedi Knight Tahl had only recently lost her sight. She was feeling helpless and angry. He remembered how Qui-Gon had quietly acknowledged her pain, then given her something to focus on.

"I'm sorry, Andra," he told her. "If we expose them, we will stop them. It's not too late."

She nodded, biting on her lip to stop the tears from falling. "Let's do it."

Her mouth set in determination, Andra turned the holographic recorder toward the pools. Obi-Wan used his recording rod to sweep the area and record the equipment. He tried to find a logo or name on various items to indicate they were owned by Offworld, but he found nothing.

Obi-Wan frowned worriedly. "We can bring this back and show it to the citizens of Thani, but we need to connect it to Xanatos. The government can claim they knew nothing about it. They can blame UniFy, and UniFy will just close its doors. Those who are truly responsible will escape."

"We can't let that happen," Andra said.

Just then they heard a noise. Someone was heading toward them. Obi-Wan gestured to Andra, and they quickly pressed themselves behind a gravsled.

Two surveillance droids rolled into view. Blasters were built into their hands. Their heads rotated constantly, infrared sensors glowing.

"All clear," one of them reported into a comlink. "Commence. Repeat, commence."

A loud noise suddenly pierced the air. The ground shook.

"What is it?" Andra asked, her hands against her ears.

"Let's take a look," Obi-Wan said. The droids had disappeared around the side of the malab slag hill.

Staying in the shadow of the hill, Obi-Wan and Andra followed. The droids were no longer in surveillance mode, so their heads no longer swiveled. As they followed, the noise grew louder.

When they rounded the pile of malab, another devastated landscape met their eyes. A mound of sand rose in front of them. A huge pit had been dug in the ground. The source of the noise was the golden sand being sucked into giant machines. Workers dressed in uni-suits tended the operation. The droids headed toward a ring of tech domes in the distance.

"There are trace minerals in the sand," Andra yelled over the noise of the machine. "They must be mining it."

The workers were intent on operating the machinery and did not turn. Andra turned on her holograph recorder and Obi-Wan his recording rod.

Another team of surveillance droids exited the first tech dome and began to make their way across the yard.

"Hurry," Obi-Wan urged. "They might switch to surveillance mode again." He lowered the recording rod and slipped it back into his tunic.

"I want to make sure the image is clear," Andra muttered.

Obi-Wan saw the infrared sensors click on. "Stop recording!" he whispered. "They might pick it up on a sensor."

"Just one more second . . ." Andra switched off the holographic recorder just as the droids' sensors began to blink.

"Don't move," Obi-Wan muttered between his teeth.

The droids' heads slowly revolved as the sensors took in every quadrant.

"This doesn't look good," Obi-Wan murmured. "Something has alerted them. We'd better get out of here."

"But we don't have enough yet!" Andra protested.

"What we have will have to do," Obi-Wan said urgently. "It will be worse if we get caught. I promised Qui-Gon we wouldn't take chances." He yanked a protesting Andra back. The droids slowly turned and headed across the yard toward them. Obi-Wan and Andra picked up their pace.

"Hurry," he urged.

Within a moment, they had ducked around the hill and were out of sight of the droids. They began to run for the cavern.

"Intruders! Intruders!"

Blaster fire suddenly ripped into the ground next to them. Obi-Wan drew his lightsaber and whirled to deflect the next blast. They were almost at the cavern entrance.

Pingpingping! The blaster fire hit the cavern wall. Chips of stone flew out, cutting Andra on the cheek.

"Get inside!" Obi-Wan shouted.

Andra ducked inside the cavern. Deflecting one last round of fire, Obi-Wan hurried after her.

They could not move as fast inside the cavern. The floor was too slippery. When they reached the velvety darkness deep inside, Obi-Wan paused.

"I don't hear anything," he said.

"Maybe they've gone for reinforcements," Andra suggested. "Come on, the exit is close by."

Obi-Wan could hear the faint murmur of the creek as he carefully followed Andra. She made her way through the maze of turns, then stopped before the sheer wall. Obi-Wan saw her flatten herself against the wall, then slip between the fissure.

They stepped out into the creek and hopped from stone to stone. They had to hurry. No doubt a full-scale alert would send other surveillance teams after them.

Obi-Wan hurried behind Andra as she snaked through the tall trees of the glade. She hugged the rock wall, then emerged where they had left their swoops.

They tossed aside the branches they had used for camouflage. The swoops were gone.

They looked at each other, stunned. There was a crack of a twig behind them, and Obi-Wan spun around.

Surveillance droids surrounded them in a semicircle, blasters drawn.

CHAPTER 13

Obi-Wan knew he was in danger even as he was turning. His turn was deliberately off center, his hand already reaching for his lightsaber in a motion so fast it was undetectable. With the other hand, he reached out and pushed Andra aside.

The blaster fire ripped between them and left a pockmarked wall.

Andra had quick reflexes. She hit the ground and kept rolling until she had reached safety behind an enormous fallen tree trunk.

Obi-Wan was seriously outnumbered. Qui-Gon's lessons snapped through his mind in precision order.

Keep moving.

Use reversals — surprise them.

Change hands when you can.

Come at them from above and below.

Use your ground.

The ground was uneven. The droids would have more trouble maneuvering. Obi-Wan used the fallen logs and soft moss beds to give him height and spring. He flipped backward and dispatched one droid with a blow to the head. Using the momentum of the swing, he dived at the next one's legs.

Two down.

Andra rose, vibroblade in hand, as Obi-Wan slashed at the third droid. Andra deftly evaded blaster fire and smashed the droid from behind.

Three down.

The fourth droid swiveled to attack Andra. Obi-Wan deflected its blaster fire with his lightsaber, then kicked out at the droid who was coming at him from the right. Andra leaped and cleaved off the droid's arm. Off-balance, the droid wobbled, and Obi-Wan was able to cleanly slice it in half. It toppled.

A vine hung down from a tree overhead, and Obi-Wan, grabbing it with one hand, used it to swing himself forward to knock over the droid who was aiming at Andra. The blaster fire erupted a split second before he swiped horizontally, cutting the droid in half.

Andra gave a cry and lay still.

Obi-Wan whirled even faster now, beheading

one droid and turning to knock another off its feet. He buried his lightsaber in the droid's control panel.

Obi-Wan rushed to Andra's side. He bent over her, feeling for her pulse.

Her hand came up, weakly swatting him away. "Don't worry, I'm not dead. I just had the wind knocked out of me."

Obi-Wan rocked back on his heels, relieved. "Are you sure?"

"The blaster fire hit my pack, I think." Gingerly, Andra slipped the pack off her shoulder. Blaster holes had shredded the material. She reached inside and took out the recorder. The case was pockmarked with blaster fire, and part of it looked melted.

"Oh, no!" she breathed. She accessed the playback mode, but the recorder merely buzzed and then went still.

"Don't worry," Obi-Wan said, patting his tunic. "That's why we brought a backup." His mind was already moving to the next step, as Qui-Gon had taught him. *Do not reflect on mishaps unless they have lessons to give.*

"Now we have another problem," he said. "Do you know any place nearby where we could get a fast transport?"

Andra paled. "No. We'd have to hike for

hours. We don't have time. Katharsis is to start in an hour. We'll never make it!"

"Let's contact Qui-Gon and see if Den was able to rig the lottery," Obi-Wan suggested. He activated the comlink. Qui-Gon answered it immediately.

"I'm glad to hear from you, Obi-Wan," he said, relief in his voice. "Did you get the evidence?"

"Not as much as we'd hoped," Obi-Wan said. "The park is definitely being developed for mining, but we have no proof that Offworld is responsible."

Qui-Gon's sigh came through the comlink. "It will have to do. I don't want to put you and Andra in any more danger."

"Was Den able to rig the lottery?"

"Yes," Qui-Gon answered. "He'll be one of the three citizens allowed to bet on the final game. He's tapped into the system and knows who the winner will be. Xanatos is delivering the grand prize."

There was a short pause. Obi-Wan felt disappointment thud through him. If only they could connect what they'd found to Offworld! They could expose Xanatos in front of the citizens he had hoodwinked.

Qui-Gon picked up on his thoughts. "Obi-Wan, you did your best. It's time to come back.

At least the global parks of Telos will be saved. Head back now."

Obi-Wan hesitated. If he told Qui-Gon that they had no transport, there was nothing Qui-Gon could do. He wouldn't have time to head out to get them and return in time for Katharsis. Telling him what had happened would only add needless worry.

"Soon," he answered instead. "We have one last thing to take care of."

"All right," Qui-Gon answered. "I'll see you at the dome. And be careful, both of you."

Andra winced. Obi-Wan signed off.

"What are you thinking?" she asked. "How can we get back to Thani?"

"We have one option," Obi-Wan said grimly. "We probably have a few minutes until they miss the droids. We have to sneak back inside and steal a transport."

Andra looked nervous, but she nodded. "It's our only chance. Let's go."

They followed the route back through the cavern. They hovered inside in the shadows of the opening, carefully waiting until a surveillance team walked through. As soon as they were gone, they slipped outside and dodged the steaming pools. They crouched behind a mole miner near the malab pile.

"What now?" Andra asked.

"I have an idea," Obi-Wan told her. "When I was plowing through those memos back at UniFy, many of them dealt with Tech Dome D. They were building a landing pad there. But I don't see one, do you? It has to be concealed inside, so it wouldn't be visible to anyone in the air. Considering the size of this operation, I'd say they were planning to bring in maintenance haulers."

Andra nodded. "Good guess."

"That means Offworld," Obi-Wan said. "They have a fleet of haulers. And they need other air transport for smaller jobs. If we can get into Tech Dome D, we can find evidence of Offworld and escape at the same time."

"So all we have to do is find Tech Dome D, then figure out how to get inside, record evidence, steal transport, and make it back to Thani before Katharsis is over," Andra said. "As Den would say, kill me now."

Obi-Wan grinned. "We can do it."

Keeping to the shadow of the malab hill and ducking out of sight when surveillance teams marched into view, Obi-Wan and Andra made their way to where they had glimpsed tech domes in the distance. Obi-Wan focused his macrobinoculars on each dome until he found Tech Dome D. He focused on its bay doors.

Workers busily walked in and out, some piloting gravsleds, some carrying durasteel bins.

When you want to leave someplace unobserved, pick the busiest spot.

"That's where we'll find transport," he told Andra.

"But the place is crawling with workers. And surveillance has been stepped up," Andra murmured. "The droids are everywhere."

"They're looking for intruders," Obi-Wan said. "Not workers."

Obi-Wan pointed to a worker exiting a small shed near them. He was fastening up his gray unisuit.

"Wait here," Obi-Wan instructed Andra.

He hugged the side of the hill of malab stone. There were only a few meters between him and the shed. He would have to chance it.

Quickly, he began to walk across the space. He gained the shelter of the door and slipped inside. A weary worker sat on a bench in front of a row of lockers. He looked up, surprised.

Obi-Wan nodded a hello. "I came for my unisuit. I'm new. Late for my shift," he added, trying to forestall any conversation.

The worker looked at him suspiciously. "The shift doesn't start for ten minutes. And you look awfully young."

Obi-Wan summoned up the Force. He directed his glance at the worker.

"But you wouldn't mind getting me a couple of suits," he said.

"Why don't I get you a couple of suits?" the worker said.

Obi-Wan took two suits from the pile the worker offered and held them up. The smaller one would fit Andra.

"See you around," he said.

"See you," the worker repeated.

Obi-Wan quickly donned the suit before exiting. He tucked the other under his arm and walked back to where Andra stood in the shadows. He handed her the unisuit and she slipped into it.

They headed for Tech Dome D. Once they got closer, Obi-Wan saw that it was three times the size of the other domes, extending back for hundreds of meters. He and Andra headed for the big double doors and strolled inside. They walked purposefully down a long aisle stacked with supply bins.

"Here, pick this up," he directed to Andra, pointing at a durasteel bin.

"Now what?" she muttered.

"Look busy." Obi-Wan scanned the area. There were several skyhoppers parked near the spaceport door. The hangar itself was big enough to park a good-sized hauler. Offworld had to be involved here.

Obi-Wan scanned the supply bins. Apparently they stored the explosive devices here. He saw a case of thermal detonators.

"Wait a second." Obi-Wan bent down to read the side of the box. Burned into the durasteel case was a broken circle.

"Offworld," he said. "We've got them!"

Andra watched for trouble while he turned the recording rod toward the cases.

They heard a noise overhead, and the roof began to retract. For a moment, the sun blazed down, then was blocked out as a huge maintenance hauler appeared. The massive ship maneuvered through the open roof and slowly lowered onto the landing bay. A moment later, a ramp slid down and workers hurriedly began unloading mole miners.

"I think we just got all the evidence we need," Obi-Wan murmured to Andra.

"Why?" she asked.

He pointed to the side of the ship. Written in laser-pulse letters along the side was OFFWORLD.

Obi-Wan panned the letters and widened his shot to take in the unloading of the mole miners. The ramps retracted. The maintenance hauler had never cut its engines. Now it fired its repulsors and began to lift off again.

"You there! Can you give us a hand?"

Two workers were busily loading supplies onto a gravsled. One of them waved a hand at Obi-Wan and Andra.

"Time to head for those skyhoppers," Obi-Wan murmured.

Obi-Wan waved back, as if he couldn't hear over the noise of the maintenance hauler's departure. Then he and Andra headed off in the other direction.

"Don't hurry," he told Andra, whose pace kept quickening, showing her anxiety.

They strolled to the skyhoppers. They had just reached them when the alarm sounded.

"Intruders," a voice intoned. "Intruders."

"Okay, *now* hurry," Obi-Wan said.

He leaped inside and Andra followed. He settled himself behind the controls as the roof began to close overhead. Obi-Wan fired up the engines. The craft rose in the air. The doors above continued to close, the opening narrowing. Obi-Wan pushed the engines to full power.

"We can't make it!" Andra screamed.

Obi-Wan yanked the controls so that the skyhopper flew sideways. He aimed for the small opening and cleared it by a centimeter on either side.

"Are we through?" Andra asked, her eyes

closed. Sweat beaded her forehead, and her hands clutched the seat.

"We're through," Obi-Wan answered. He wiped the sweat off his own forehead with his sleeve. "Next stop, Thani."

CHAPTER 14

Qui-Gon paced impatiently near the central ring of the dome. He was careful to keep his hood forward to conceal his face. The mid-game break was taking place, and much of the crowd had headed for the food stalls, but he couldn't take a chance of being spotted. His picture was on every information kiosk in Thani.

Obi-Wan and Andra should have been back by now. What if something had happened to Obi-Wan? This was the second time the boy had been in great danger. Again, Qui-Gon had allowed it to happen.

"Settle down, Qui-Gon," Den said. "You're making me nervous." But Qui-Gon noted that Den's face was taut with nerves, and he continually scanned the aisles around them.

"You're worried about Andra, too," Qui-Gon said.

"Who, me?" Den said, turning away. "I don't

worry about other people. Only myself. I'm the one who's about to bet his life savings."

Once Den had rigged the results so that he could win the lottery, he had to come up with the resources to make a credible bet. Den had added all the credits he had to one of the many easy loans available on Telos. If he lost, he would be liable for a heavy debt.

"Are you certain you interpreted the game correctly?" Qui-Gon asked. "You're sure you know who will win?"

"I'll get my legs broken if I'm wrong," Den said. "It's Kama Elias. Relax."

"Remember, after you win, I'll be right here," Qui-Gon advised him. "Don't even entertain the possibility of taking off with that prize. That money is going straight back into the treasury of Telos."

"Of course it is," Den said. "Kill me now if you think I'd double-cross my friends."

"Don't tempt me," Qui-Gon said dryly.

The dais in the central ring began to rise, signaling the start of the next round of games. Qui-Gon and Den took their seats. Qui-Gon kept an eye out for Obi-Wan. After the lottery winners bet on the final contest, Xanatos would present the prize. Then scenes of what Katharsis funded would flash on the giant screens. Instead of images of pristine beauty, the crowd would see scenes of devastation. But only if Obi-Wan returned in time.

The second round of games began. The battered contestants now played a round of shock ball. Roars from the crowd encouraged the most savage play.

Qui-Gon's worry intensified. Where was Obi-Wan?

He remembered the circumstances of their leaving the Temple. They had stood together on the landing platform, ready to take a shuttle to the spaceliner port. They had already said good-bye to their friends, to Tahl and Bant and Garen. They had said good-bye to a disapproving Yoda.

"It is not too late, Obi-Wan," Qui-Gon had said. "There will be no shame if you remain here. It will not interfere with what happens with us later. I promise you that. It is better for you if you stay."

He remembered the clear resolution in Obi-Wan's gaze. "I can't say that you need me, Qui-Gon. I know you can do this on your own. But I will help."

Now Qui-Gon admonished himself. He had thought then that he could not prevent Obi-Wan from coming. He had taken the resolution in the boy's gaze to mean that even if he insisted, Obi-

Wan would not walk back into the Temple and remain.

But was that true? Was his own quiet gratitude what had been most important at that moment? Again, it was his own emotion that had swayed him. Should he have taken a firm stance and insisted Obi-Wan remain? Had he been selfish?

Qui-Gon nearly groaned aloud. Obi-Wan was not officially his Padawan again, yet he kept coming up against the many ways he could fail him. He had been reluctant to shoulder the responsibility of a new Padawan in the first place. Then he had come to accept it. Soon he had taken pleasure from that responsibility. And now he was at sea with it. Adrift with his feelings, wanting to do the right thing and not quite sure how. All too aware of his own failings, all too aware of what could go wrong.

Yet Obi-Wan was so sure. The boy still had things to teach him about certainty. About trust.

If only he would show up.

Qui-Gon caught a glimpse of a familiar form moving quickly through the crowd. Obi-Wan! Andra hurried by his side, taking quick steps to keep up with Obi-Wan's stride. He knew with a glance at Obi-Wan's face that his mission had been successful.

Obi-Wan and Andra slipped past a row of protesting onlookers to reach Den and Qui-Gon. Obi-Wan handed the recording rod to Qui-Gon.

"We got it all," he said.

Qui-Gon immediately rose and hurried off. He had already discovered the booth where the technician who transmitted the visual images to the crowd during the breaks was located.

The technician sat at a console, eating a greasy meat pie. Around him were tiny screens that showed what was currently playing to the crowd. One camera was on each contestant, one took in a full view, several took partial views, and the rest scanned the faces in the crowd. During the break, all of these would be replaced with the global park images.

The technician looked up. "Who're you?"

Qui-Gon placed the recording rod on the console. "These images are to be shown after Xanatos' speech. Governor's orders."

The technician licked a drop of sauce off his thumb. "I didn't hear anything about this."

Qui-Gon directed his gaze at the man, who continued to eat. "You should show the images after the speech."

"I'll show them after the speech," the technician said, his mouth full.

Qui-Gon eyed his greasy fingers. "And you'll clean your hands first."

"I'll clean my hands first," the technician said, as if he'd just thought of it.

Qui-Gon waited until the technician tossed his food away and carefully wiped his fingers. Then he watched him load the new visuals. When he was sure the man would follow through on the plan, he left.

The last game had ended. Only four contestants remained.

The governor announced the names of the lottery winners. A mixture of groans and cheers erupted from the crowd. When he announced Den's name, Den shot to his feet, yodeling wildly.

He turned back to them, his eyes alight. "Ready?"

Andra's gaze was steady. "Do not fail us, Den."

Den leaned over. "You've got to trust somebody sometime, Captain Integrity," he said softly.

"I know," Andra said. "But why does it have to be you?"

Then she smiled at him, a smile filled with trust. She briefly touched his cheek.

A slow, delighted smile spread over Den's boyish features. Still grinning, he strode off to join the other lottery winners onstage. Andra clasped her hands together.

"I trust him, too," Qui-Gon told her.

Obi-Wan shot him a look that asked, *How can you be sure?*

Qui-Gon wanted to tell him that sometimes he found it easier to read strangers than those close to him. When his heart wasn't involved, his instincts told him who could fail him, who would be true. He hoped that after this mission, he and Obi-Wan would have time to talk.

Obi-Wan leaned closer to him. "Are you certain about this?"

Qui-Gon nodded. "Yes, I am. But I also have swoops ready in case he takes off. Over the years, I've learned to back up my instincts."

The lottery contestants stood at small consoles. They wagered enormous sums on the final outcome. Den made a show of indecisive agony before placing his bet. Andra sighed.

"He can't resist a chance to show off," she said, her hands twisting nervously.

The final round began. It was a short replay of each of the games that had been played throughout the contest. By now the contestants were covered with sweat, grime, and blood. Each of the lottery winners sat on a dais, watching the action, knowing that their life savings depended on the outcome. This was the time that the crowd kept up one continuous roar.

The game of shock ball ended the match.

Kama Elias suddenly zoomed past his opponent, who turned too sharply and spiraled out of control, taking a bad fall. Kama scored. The buzzer sounded. The games were over.

Den leaped off the dais and did a frenzied dance in the middle of the arena. The crowd loved it, screaming his name. The screens flashed DEN DEN DEN!!!!

Then the platform slowly rose from the center ring, and Xanatos stood, a commanding figure in black. He raised his arms to the crowd and the chant changed to his name. Thousands of feet pounded against the floor until the entire dome shuddered. XAN-A-TOS! XAN-A-TOS! XAN-A-TOS!

He raised a hand for quiet. Slowly, the cheers subsided. Then, his hypnotic voice boomed over the dome.

"Katharsis saves us!"

"YES!" the crowd responded.

"Katharsis enriches us!"

"YES!"

"Katharsis protects our sacred spaces!"

"YES!"

Qui-Gon looked up at the screens. *Do it now,* he urged the technician.

The scenes of the frenzied crowd disappeared. An image of the Sacred Pools took its place. But instead of the glittering crystal water, a foamy black pool appeared. Steam rose from the surface.

At first, the crowd didn't notice. Then another image flashed, and another. The hill of malab slabs. Mole miners. The scan grid lying near shattered stone. Giant machines sucking golden sand. Gravsleds parked on a once-pristine landscape.

Murmurs began. Xanatos did not notice them. His eyes were on the crowd, not the giant screens.

"Thanks to Katharsis, our beloved Telos is now ensured protection for generations," he said. "The people have spoken. They have safeguarded their legacy."

An image of the Offworld logo filled the screen. It was burned into a case of thermal detonators.

The murmurs of the restless crowd turned to a buzz of conversation that filled the dome like a room full of tech equipment gone haywire.

The next image was of mole miners being unloaded from the maintenance hauler. An image filled the screen: OFFWORLD.

The buzz turned into a roar of disbelief and anger.

Xanatos looked up at the screens at last. Qui-Gon watched him. Anyone else would have shown his surprise and anger. Xanatos just went still.

Shouting erupted around the dome. Many rose to their feet. The shouts rose in intensity. People began to stand on their chairs and raise their fists. A rhythmic pounding began, a demand more potent than a shouted question.

Xanatos raised his hands, motioning for silence. It took several moments for the crowd to quiet down.

"Why do you believe what you see?" he asked in a quiet, commanding tone. "Believe what I tell you. Someone is trying to inflame you. Someone is trying to trick you."

A lone voice arose from the crowd. "Is it you?"

The crowd took up the question. "IS IT YOU? IS IT YOU?"

"We demand an answer!" someone else shouted.

"I am answering your doubts!" Xanatos thundered. "I am telling you that there is trickery afoot here! And I invite anyone in the crowd to come with me to the Sacred Pools and examine what is there. I trust my government. I trust the UniFy corporation. Governor, will you allow the Sacred Pools to be opened to the public to see for themselves?"

A silver-haired man rose from the front row of the dome. "I will."

Xanatos spread his hands. "You see? There is no deviousness here. There is only openness. We will prevail if we do not fall for tricks."

The crowd began to quiet. Trust was winning out over anger.

"Now let me bring those who have lied to our beloved world to justice!" Xanatos shouted, and the crowd roared its approval.

Xanatos stepped away from the platform for a moment. Qui-Gon saw him speak rapidly to one of the security police ringing the arena. He saw one of them speak into a comlink.

Dread filled Qui-Gon. "Put your hood up, Obi-Wan," he said quickly.

Moments later, the faces of Qui-Gon and Obi-Wan flashed onscreen.

"Have you seen these men?" Xanatos boomed. He pointed to the screens. "They are enemies of Telos! Condemned to death, they escaped and now continue to work their evil! They are here, in this arena. They are the ones who switched the image tapes. Look at your neighbors. Do you see them? They are the ones who tricked you!"

"Uh-oh," Andra breathed. She leaned forward, shielding Obi-Wan and Qui-Gon by pretending to search the crowd around her.

But it was no use. A Telosian in front of them turned and peered beneath their hoods. Surprise and recognition made his mouth drop. Then, he stood and screamed out, "Here! Here they are!"

There was no chance to move, and nowhere to go. Security police poured down the aisles and Obi-Wan and Qui-Gon were caught.

CHAPTER 15

The security police dragged Obi-Wan and Qui-Gon into the aisle. They surrounded them with blasters drawn. Two of them held Qui-Gon by the arms, two more held Obi-Wan.

"Hey!" Den shouted from the stage. "Enough of this. I won! Where's my prize?"

The crowd took up the cry. This is what they waited for — to see the winner accept a fortune in credits and crystalline vertex. Even the security police wanted to see it. Although their blasters stayed leveled at the Jedi, their eyes darted to the stage.

Xanatos hurriedly strode forward, a transparent box in his hands. Crystals glittered inside and credits spilled from the top. Xanatos seemed visibly anxious to get the ceremony over with, Obi-Wan noted.

Xanatos handed the box to Den. Everyone

turned toward him. It was customary for the winner to say a few words.

Den stood, looking at the box. He did not speak.

Obi-Wan glanced at Qui-Gon. This was the test. Things had changed. They were in custody. Den could see that. Andra could not stop him alone. If Den didn't follow through on their plan, he could keep a fortune. The amount in the box would tempt almost any being, let alone a thief.

Instead of addressing the crowd, Den turned and spoke to the tall, silver-haired man in the first tier of seats. "Governor?"

The Governor of Telos stood.

"Will you read the durasheet I handed you before the final contest took place?"

The Governor reached into the pocket of his tunic. He leaned over and read into the amplification device. "The winner will be Kama Elias by twenty points. Deleta will experience a steering problem. Kama will push past to win."

The crowd looked on, mystified. Kama had won by twenty points. But how did the winner know that Deleta would have a steering problem?

"Citizens of Telos, I wrote that before the games began," Den announced. "I broke into the Katharsis computer. Every Katharsis contest is rigged! The equipment of the contestants is subtly altered as the games go on so that the prechosen winner will triumph. Even the winner of the lottery is chosen ahead of time. The winner must agree to split the fortune with UniFy. This whole thing is a setup designed to get your money!"

Den reached into the box and withdrew fistfuls of credits and crystalline vertex. He tossed them to the crowd. The credits and vertex rained down, and people scrambled to pick them up. Around them the screens flashed images of the devastated Sacred Pools.

"They've lied to us!" he shouted. "Look at the screens! *This* is what your money has bought! Look around you — look at each other. Are you in debt? Do you only think about money? Good — because that's what they want! And while we scheme and dream, our world is being destroyed. Look at the logo on those crates of explosives, on that ship. UniFy is Offworld! Our planet has been sold to the biggest mining corporation in the galaxy while we bet on a *game.* And who runs Offworld? The mighty Xanatos!"

For a moment, the collective silence of the crowd seemed to suck all the air out of the dome. Then the silence broke into a great roar, as mighty as the sea.

The security police holding Obi-Wan were just as transfixed as the crowd. The crowd rose as one body, leaping to its feet and screaming for Xanatos. The screen still flashed image after image of the ravaged park.

"Arrest him!" they shouted. "Arrest Xanatos!"

Xanatos stepped forward once again. He waited out the shouts and jeers. Slowly, people in the crowd began to hush one another. Everyone expected Xanatos to calm them again. To tell them that what Den was saying was a lie.

Xanatos surveyed the crowd for a long moment, waiting out every murmur until the dome was silent once more.

Then, he smiled and shook his head like a teacher admonishing a class of students. "You pathetic fools."

Moving astonishingly fast, his cloak streaming behind him, he leaped onto the winner's swoop. He rose into the air, pushing the swoop to maximum speed. Weaving to avoid the floating boxes, he expertly maneuvered the craft out of the dome toward the exit.

"Not this time, Xanatos," Qui-Gon said grimly.

It was easy to break the holds of the distracted guards. Obi-Wan struck out with his elbow and knee, freeing himself. Afraid to fire their blasters in the midst of the weaving, angered crowd, the guards could not catch up to them.

Qui-Gon had hidden their swoops behind a stack of benches. They leaped on them and took off in the direction Xanatos had gone.

CHAPTER 16

By the time they roared out of the dome, the boulevard seemed completely empty. Qui-Gon closed his eyes for a moment and focused. When he opened them again, he caught the flicker of movement down the street to his right. Perhaps it was just a shadow. But the Force told him it was Xanatos.

Qui-Gon pushed his engines as high as they would go. He could hear Obi-Wan directly behind him. The boy would keep up. He knew that.

Determination tightened every muscle. He would not lose Xanatos now. No doubt he was heading somewhere he would be safe, or perhaps toward transport off-planet. Xanatos always had an escape route.

But they had taken him by surprise. Perhaps there were details left to arrange. Xanatos could not have prepared for this.

To Qui-Gon's surprise, Xanatos headed out of the city and took off over open country.

"I think he's heading to the Sacred Pools," Obi-Wan shouted. "This is the way we went."

"We'll have to stay behind him," Qui-Gon answered. "He knows we're following him. If we can't catch him, we can keep him in sight."

The swoop engines could only be pushed so far. Xanatos had a faster craft, since the ones used for the games had modified engines. The Jedi could barely manage to keep him in sight, and there were stretches where they lost him completely.

Over the course of the ride, Obi-Wan never lost his focus. He settled in over the handlebars, his eyes trained on the speck in the distance that was Xanatos. Qui-Gon's face was set in determined lines.

At last they reached the road to the park. They roared down it, heading for the entrance. The gate was formed from electrowire. Sensors were aimed above to blast any vehicles flying over it.

A swoop lay abandoned on the road. Xanatos was nowhere in sight.

Qui-Gon pulled his swoop over. He examined the swoop on the ground. It was out of fuel.

"He must be in the park," he said. He eyed the gate.

"I have another way in," Obi-Wan assured him.

Obi-Wan led the way back down the road through the trees. He left his swoop and splashed through the creek toward the fissure in the cavern wall. He pressed himself inside.

Qui-Gon followed with difficulty. He was a big man, and it was a small crack. Somehow he was able to push himself through.

They quickly made their way to the entrance of the cavern and burst out into the open air. Xanatos was crossing the yard, heading for Tech Dome D.

"There's a landing pad inside," Obi-Wan told Qui-Gon. "No doubt he has transport off-planet waiting there."

Qui-Gon began to run. Xanatos must never reach the Tech Dome.

He moved silently, his feet not making even a whisper of sound on the soft ground. But before he could reach Xanatos, his opponent suddenly leaped on a gravsled and took off.

Qui-Gon grabbed an abandoned gravsled and followed, knowing Obi-Wan would be only moments behind him. He maneuvered around a pile of equipment and managed to cut Xanatos off from the tech dome. With a snarl, Xanatos wheeled the gravsled, making a sharp right and zooming off. Qui-Gon was on his tail.

Ahead lay a ravaged landscape. The lowering sun painted it with bloodred rays. Steaming pools of black acid bubbled and sent vapor into the air. The area was lumpy with hardened lava and sticky with tar. The air seemed thick and yellow with chemicals. Occasionally a large burst of steam erupted from fissures in the rock.

Xanatos flew off the gravsled. He landed on his feet, lightsaber in hand, perfectly positioned to attack. Taken off guard, Qui-Gon turned the gravsled too rapidly. He felt the vehicle was close to overturning and he jumped off.

The leap was awkward, but it saved him. He felt Xanatos' lightsaber buzz near his ear as it came down and struck rock.

Qui-Gon landed off balance and on one knee, but his lightsaber was activated and in his hand, ready to ward off the next blow. The tubes of light met and tangled, buzzing and sending a charge into the air.

"You won't kill me, Qui-Gon," Xanatos said, their faces close. His blue eyes burned with hatred.

"I am not here to kill you," Qui-Gon said. "I am here to bring you to justice." He somersaulted backward and reversed direction, hoping to knock the lightsaber from his opponent's hand.

The blow came down, but Xanatos met it and twisted away.

"Tell the truth for once, Qui-Gon," he sneered. "You spend so much time mouthing those Jedi pieces of wisdom that you've lost touch with your honesty, if you ever had it at all. You won't be satisfied until I'm dead. Look, here comes your young puppet."

Qui-Gon saw the blue glow of Obi-Wan's lightsaber as the boy rushed toward them. He sensed Obi-Wan would move to the right. If they flanked Xanatos, perhaps they could disarm him.

They moved at the same split second without exchanging a glance. Qui-Gon knew when and how Obi-Wan would strike, with a downward blow at the hilt of the lightsaber. Qui-Gon dropped to one knee for an upward strike. It would be difficult for Xanatos to counter both blows.

But Xanatos had anticipated their moves. He whirled away from Obi-Wan's blow and leaped backward, using the Force to add distance to the jump. Qui-Gon struck upward but only dealt a glancing blow to Xanatos' lightsaber. A fissure exploded near him, the steam hissing upward in a powerful column. He had to leap aside to avoid being scalded.

The steam column separated the Jedi from Xanatos, who smiled.

"Here we go again," Xanatos said. "The noble Jedi try to pretend they only come for justice when actually they come for blood. Remember, Obi-Wan? You took off after a thirteen-year-old boy and then he turned up dead. Do you remember the look in Bruck's eyes when you killed him? Are you trying to tell yourself that you're sorry your rival is dead? Admit the feeling in your heart. Admit your gladness! Admit your thirst for revenge."

Qui-Gon saw the distress in Obi-Wan's face. The hand holding the lightsaber trembled.

"Don't listen," he said quietly. "Don't listen, Obi-Wan."

The steam was sucked back into the fissure. At the same moment, Xanatos leaped forward. Still shaken, Obi-Wan was caught off guard. He barely was able to parry Xanatos' blow with his lightsaber. Xanatos whirled, one leg kicking out, sending Obi-Wan flying backward.

Then Xanatos leaped after the fallen boy.

CHAPTER 17

"No!" Qui-Gon cried. He reached out to the rocks and vegetation that surrounded him, for the current that connected him to all things, that connected him to Obi-Wan.

He hit Xanatos in midair. Their bodies connected like mountains of hard rock. There was no give to Xanatos' muscles, no yielding in Qui-Gon. The clash was titanic. Qui-Gon felt the shock of it move through his bones. For a moment, Xanatos gripped Qui-Gon's arm, forcing them to remain entangled.

"You brought me to this," he said, his midnight eyes burning.

They landed inches apart, lightsabers already engaged. The lava was slippery and Qui-Gon had to avoid the fissures of steam. He saw Obi-Wan beginning to struggle to his feet.

"So the pupil has learned from the teacher," Xanatos went on relentlessly. "Lie about your feelings while you talk of Jedi honor. Leave murder in your wake."

"You are responsible for Bruck's death," Qui-Gon told him as they fought. "Not Obi-Wan. You corrupted the boy, exposed him to the dark side. He followed you blindly."

Obi-Wan limped slightly as he headed toward them. He had turned his ankle. His face still looked naked and young, still stung by what Xanatos had flung at him.

Qui-Gon thought that Obi-Wan had come to terms with what had happened. He had regretted and mourned Bruck's death, for even though Bruck had done evil, there was still hope for him while he was alive. Obi-Wan had not seemed to blame himself.

Yet somewhere inside, he had. A life had been ended. That was a loss not easily absorbed. Qui-Gon knew that well. And Xanatos would see that hesitancy in Obi-Wan, and would use it to taunt him. He would see weakness where Qui-Gon saw strength. Such was the nature of evil.

Courage, Obi-Wan. Grab your conviction. Know what you know. Do not let him reach you.

"I see my words have touched you, Obi-Wan," Xanatos said in the silky, insinuating tone he used to manipulate those around him. "Can it be because I'm right?"

"No, Xanatos," Obi-Wan said. "I grieve for a life lost. And I thank all who taught me for my grief. It does not make me weak. It makes me strong."

Suddenly, Obi-Wan's lightsaber whirled. Qui-Gon was astonished at how quickly and gracefully the boy moved, leaping off a mound of lava to strike at Xanatos. Xanatos stumbled backward from the ferocity of the attack. A cloud of steam suddenly erupted, and he quickly lurched to one side, losing his balance and landing on one hand.

"Stronger than you," Obi-Wan added fiercely, leaping after him.

Qui-Gon followed, admiring Obi-Wan's focus. Now the two fought as one. Xanatos had weakened, and they used this to drive him back, back against the black pool. If they could get his back against it, they would be able to disarm him or defeat him. It would be his choice.

Two swoops suddenly appeared from behind the pool. Andra and Den had found them. They landed and ran to help, their blasters at the ready.

"You will pay, Xanatos!" Andra shouted. "We will take you back to Thani for trial!"

Xanatos stood at the edge of the water behind him. He had no hope of escape. He was surrounded, and there was nowhere to run to.

His gaze traveled from Den to Andra to Obi-Wan, finally resting on Qui-Gon. The depths of his hatred turned his gaze as black and foul as the steaming pool.

"You will never have the satisfaction of killing me, Qui-Gon Jinn," he said softly. "And I will never submit to anyone's laws. Your hate drove you, though you won't admit it. You destroyed me because you could not save me. I am your biggest failure. Live with that. And live with this."

"No!" Qui-Gon cried, starting forward.

But he was too late. With a cruel smile that stretched his lips over his teeth like an animal, Xanatos took two quick steps backward and leaped into the boiling black pool. Andra cried out as he disappeared.

"He can't survive," she whispered. "The acid will strip the flesh off his bones."

Obi-Wan shuddered. He had seen what the pool could do. Xanatos was pure evil. But he was a living being, and he had gone to a horrible fate. Qui-Gon seemed frozen, staring at the murky, stinking pool.

Slowly, something stirred in the water, spiraling upward. It was a black cape. As they watched, it disintegrated before their eyes.

Xanatos was dead at last.

CHAPTER 18

Den stretched his arms over his head and smiled. "Whoever would have thought that a thief and a dinko would be the grand heroes of Telos?"

Andra threw a pillow at him. "I'm glad all the attention hasn't gone to your head."

Obi-Wan and Qui-Gon smiled, used to Den and Andra's squabbling by now. They knew a deep affection was growing between the two.

Their return to Telos had brought everything Andra had wanted for so long. UniFy had been exposed as a front for Offworld. Their treacherous activities had come to light. The government had apologized to the people, then called for special elections. Investigations had begun into payoffs to various government heads. The governor who had turned a blind eye had resigned. The treasurer, Vox Chun, was in jail.

And Katharsis had been stopped. The citizens

of Telos were horrified that they had been hoodwinked by greed. Mass delirium had taken over, they claimed. Scores of citizens had contacted Andra, hoping to join the POWER party. A new patriotism had flared on Telos, one based on commitment and stewardship of the land they cherished and had almost lost forever.

"So what kind of governor do you think I'd make?" Den asked. "The people love me."

"That's because they don't know you like we do," Andra said with a grin. "You're no politician, Den."

"Hey, you yourself said I was good at lying," Den protested, pretending to be hurt.

"There will be no more lying by a government on Telos, ever again," Andra said seriously.

"I'd take that bet, but I don't like the odds," Den added more cynically.

Qui-Gon rose. "I wish you both luck. And we thank you for helping to clear up those charges."

"You're free to go, but must you?" Andra asked. "We'd love you to stay for a few days. Let me show you the beauties of Telos. The Sacred Pools will take time to clean up, but there are other places."

"Some other time. We must return to the Temple."

Obi-Wan rose and thanked Andra and Den. He was sorry to say good-bye. He admired Andra's commitment. He had been suspicious of Den, but he had come to appreciate him, too. He knew that in their different ways, they would work to restore Telos to the busy, peaceful, blooming world it had been.

"I know we're leaving Telos in good hands," Obi-Wan told them. He grinned at Den. "I'd say the odds are definitely in your favor."

Obi-Wan walked with Qui-Gon down the wide boulevard toward the spaceliner that would take them back to Coruscant.

"Was Xanatos your biggest failure?" he asked tentatively. "Will his death haunt you, as he hoped?"

"Does Bruck's death haunt you?" Qui-Gon asked softly.

"No," Obi-Wan said slowly. "But I carry it here." He touched his chest.

"It is the same for me, I think," Qui-Gon said. "It will not haunt me — not the way Xanatos hoped it would. Xanatos chose death. It was his nature to choose the dark path. But it will take some time for me to feel peace about it. I cannot help feeling that if I'd been a better Master, he wouldn't have turned to the Dark Side. Yoda would tell me that as a Master, I cannot make a Padawan a success or a failure. I can only guide."

And me? Obi-Wan wanted to ask. *How do you see me, Qui-Gon — success, or failure?*

Qui-Gon didn't speak for a few minutes. He seemed to devote himself to enjoying the beauty of the day, as though he needed it to chase away sorrow.

"You are just beginning your journey, Obi-Wan," he said at last. "Do not concern yourself with success or failure. If you act rightly, those words lose their meaning. There is only the good that you do."

"It's hard not to think of failure, considering I've been put on probation," Obi-Wan said.

"That has nothing to do with failure," Qui-Gon said gently. "You must not think it does. The Jedi path is a difficult one to walk. The Council knows this. If someone strays, especially at a young age, they understand. But still they must be certain of your commitment. You will have to meet with them, spend time at the Temple renewing your dedication. It will be a good thing for both of us, I think. There is a time for missions. And then there is a time for meditation and study."

"You will be at the Temple too?" Obi-Wan asked.

Qui-Gon nodded. "It is time for reflection for me as well. And I will help you with the Council. They must understand why you made the decision to leave. I have come to understand it."

"You have?"

"I was slow to do so, I admit," Qui-Gon said. "But yes, I have." He paused. "I know you are on probation and can't be my official apprentice. But you are my Padawan, Obi-Wan. I do not need the Council to tell me so."

Obi-Wan took a deep breath. "Then you'll take me back?"

"We will take each other back," Qui-Gon said.

Obi-Wan had hoped for this. He had tried to control his impatience for it. Now here it was, and he found he had no words. He was too deeply moved to form them.

"I fought our bond from the first," Qui-Gon said. "But you knew something I didn't. You knew that some things are meant to be. Now I know it, too. You will make a fine Jedi Knight. I would be proud to continue the journey we started together."

Obi-Wan lifted his head. Now he, too, saw the beauty of the day. The sky was dazzlingly clear. For the first time in what felt like a long while, the future was clear as well.

"I am not saying the way will be easy," Qui-

Gon added. "We have different temperaments. No doubt we will clash. You will come to challenge me again."

"I will try not to," Obi-Wan told him earnestly.

"You don't understand, Padawan." Qui-Gon gave the smile he gave so rarely, a full smile that lit up his blue eyes and caused them to sparkle with warmth. "I look forward to it."

Tal has lived his whole life in darkness. He has never left his home, a mysterious castle of seven towers. But Tal cannot stay safe forever. When his family and his life are threatened, he must do anything he can in order to obtain a rare and magical Sunstone. He even takes on an Imperial Guard named Ethar in a fierce game called Beastmaker . . .

Tal sat down at the game table, and Ethar sat opposite. Tal felt strangely calm now that he had accepted the challenge. He looked down at the seven rectangular depressions in the tabletop in front of him. He knew what they were, but he thought he'd pretend to know less about the game. That way Ethar might underestimate him.

"What order are these in again?" he asked, pointing to the rectangles.

"Head, Heart, Temper, Skin, Speed, Strength, and Special," said Ethar quickly.

Each rectangle would ultimately hold one card, and that card would specify the characteristics of the beast. The Strength card would determine the beast's strength, the speed card would determine its quickness, and so on. When all the cards were in place and finalized, two five-inch high beasts of solid light would be produced, to battle it out in the marble circle in the middle of the table. Whoever played their cards right and produced the victorious beast would win the game.

Each card could be changed twice by using light. So even when a card was in place, and your opponent could see it, it might still change. The trick of the game was to make the other player think you were making a certain sort of beast and then change it at the last moment by altering the cards that governed its seven characteristics.

There was also luck, of course. There were a hundred cards, but each player was only dealt seven, all of which had three possible variations.

Tal hoped that he would be lucky.

Tal's first card was a Phalarope, a marine animal that floated around in the water and had thousands of poisonous tendrils. Its only real use was in the Special category, because then the made beast would have poisonous tendrils. Tal knew that this card would change to a Kurshken if he applied green light from his Sunstone. Kurshken were small but very smart and quick lizards, so it would be good in either Speed or Head.

Unfortunately, Tal didn't know what the third variation of the card was. He had a faint memory that it might turn into a Hugthing under red light, but couldn't be sure. Hugthings were particularly nasty. They looked like a carpet of comfortable green moss, but could spring up and wrap themselves around you in an instant. For the game, a Hugthing card would be good in Skin or Strength.

"I will play first, if you like," said Ethar. This would give Tal a slight advantage, so he quickly nodded to say yes.

"Heart of a Borzog," announced Ethar, laying the card down on the second rectangle in front of her. Tal looked at the card, which showed a fearsome, semi-human and very hairy creature roughly the size of three people across the shoulders. This was a good initial play. Borzogs would fight to the death and beyond. Once they got a grip, they never let go, even when they were killed. Strong-hearted indeed.

Um, err, Head of a . . . whatever this is . . ." announced Tal, playing the Phalarope into the Head rectangle. He was going to change it into a Kurshken later on, but he hoped Ethar would think he didn't know what he was doing.

"A Phalarope," said Ethar. She looked at the bulbous thing with its many tentacles and added, "It does look something like a giant brain."

"That's what I thought," said Tal, pretending he was relieved. "A giant brain. Perfect for the Head."

The other guard dealt them both another card. Tal picked his up slowly. At first, all he could see was a pair of red eyes in the card. Then, he slowly became aware of an outline around them. The card was showing him something hidden in a cave or a hole, with only the eyes visible.

Then Tal remembered, and barely suppressed a shiver of horror. This card was of a Cavernmouth. They were horrible creatures in Aenir, who dug holes for themselves in the sides of mountains and then backed in and opened their enormous jaws. What he thought were glowing eyes were actually something like tonsils at the back of the thing's throat.

In the game of Beastmaker, the Cavernmouth card was unusual. It could be played in Speed, because its jaws were incredibly fast at snapping out. Or it could be played in Special, to give the created beast extendable jaws.

"Speed of a Gorblag," said Ethar, playing a card that looked like a large, glowing blue toad that was too fat to do anything. But one of the variation of the Gorblag card was the incredibly zappy Fleamite, an insect that could move faster than a human eye could track it. Tal knew Ethar would change that card later on.

"Speed of a Cavernmouth," Tal countered, playing his card. He wouldn't be changing that. Even if Ethar did change her Speed card to the Fleamite, it wouldn't be much faster than a Cavernmouth.

"You have played before," remarked Ethar. "Few people remember the Cavernmouth can be played for Speed."

"I saw my great-uncle use it that way once," Tal said, still trying to give the impression he was an absolute beginner at Beastmaker.

The game moved more swiftly then. Within a few minutes, both Tal and Ethar had six of their seven rectangles filled with cards.

"You hid your skill well," said Ethar as she

changed the mild-mannered Klatha workbeast in her Temper rectangle to the insanely vicious Vengenarl, a creature that attacked even its own kind if they trespassed over its scent-marked boundaries.

Tal nodded, but he wasn't paying attention to what Ethar said. Everything depended on him getting the best beast. Now Ethar had changed the Temper of her beast, Tal thought he knew what to play there. But once he put that card down, his beast would be complete. Did he need to make any changes?

Quickly, he scanned the seven rectangles. Head of a Kurshken. Skin of a Samheal Semidragon. Temper . . . that was to come. Heart of a Hrugen, which was a gamble, since that was actually a kind of weed that never gave up, it grew everywhere in Aenir and seemingly could not be eradicated. Speed of a Cavernmouth. Strength of a Jarghoul, a cannibalistic strangling snake of the jungles of Aenir that primarily ate others of its own kind after weeks-long battles to crush each other to death. Special, the ability of the Gossamer Bug to fly.

Tal ran over the variations in his head, while Ethar arched her fingers into a steeple and waited for his move.

"To see the Empress, or lose your Sunstone," she said. "What is it to be?"

"Temper of an Icefang," said Tal, playing his final card, locking all the others in. This was his greatest gamble. He didn't know enough about this card or its properties. But he remembered Great-Uncle Ebbitt saying that the Icefangs of Aenir were among the most dangerous of creatures in the spirit world. They never got angry, or demoralized, or had any emotions at all it seemed. They just coldly fought to the very best of their ability, never distracted by danger, wounds, or anything else.

"And Strength of a . . . Jarghoul," said Ethar, playing exactly the same card as Tal. "Let the battle begin!"

The Early Adventures of
Obi-Wan Kenobi and Qui-Gon Jinn

STAR WARS®

JEDI APPRENTICE

- BDN 0-590-51922-0 #1: The Rising Force $4.99 US
- BDN 0-590-51925-5 #2: The Dark Rival $4.99 US
- BDN 0-590-51933-6 #3: The Hidden Past $4.99 US
- BDN 0-590-51934-4 #4: The Mark of the Crown $4.99 US
- BDN 0-590-51956-5 #5: The Defenders of the Dead $4.99 US
- BDN 0-590-51969-7 #6: The Uncertain Path $4.99 US
- BDN 0-590-51970-0 #7: The Captive Temple $4.99 US
- BDN 0-590-52079-2 #8: The Day of Reckoning $4.99 US

Also available:

- BDN 0-439-52093-8 *Star Wars Journal:*
  Episode I: Anakin Skywalker $5.99 US
- BDN 0-439-52101-2 *Star Wars Journal:*
  Episode I: Queen Amidala $5.99 US
- BDN 0-439-13941-4 *Star Wars Journal:*
  Episode I:—Darth Maul $5.99 US
- BDN 0-439-01089-1 *Star Wars: Episode I—*
  The Phantom Menace $5.99 US

Scholastic Inc., P.O. Box 7502, Jefferson City, MO 65102

Please send me the books I have checked above. I am enclosing $_____ (please add $2.00 to cover shipping and handling). Send check or money order–no cash or C.O.D.s please.

Name_____Birthdate_____

Address_____

City_____State/Zip_____

Please allow four to six weeks for delivery. Offer good in U.S.A. only. Sorry, mail orders are not available to residents of Canada. Prices subject to change.

SWA1199

Visit us at www.scholastic.com